DEATH

THE PHARMACIST

DEATH

THE PHARMACIST

D. IKE HORST

atmosphere press

TABLE OF CONTENTS

CHAPTER **ONE**

Death, the Pharmacist, stood assertively behind a smooth counter of deep ebony with his hands, resplendent in powdery blue gloves, gripped tightly behind his back. His chin tilted proudly upward, angular shoulders pronounced.

He looked out.

Amid the ever-white way station that was his pharmacy, just beyond the solid black countertop that acted as a border to a bright pigmentless canvas, an orderly line of drudge life-forms came in countless waves. They moved automatically, as though they were ushered along by a conveyor belt. These gray-shaded beings were merely figments of humans, beasts, and other life—all of them waiting their turn at Death's counter.

Their presence was constant, thankfully neat, but constant. Death couldn't imagine the chaos that would ensue if they moved with free will, especially when he considered the sheer number of them. These beings appeared day after day to pick up their daily dose of life essence, and it was a single-minded pursuit that required nothing but the innate desire to continue one's existence.

One such creature appeared. A venerable human male stood at the head of the line, just beyond the threshold, lifeless eyes reaching for the empty receptacle assigned to him—a container which was void of the brilliant cobalt life essence orbs that the man was conditioned to seek.

Death moved until he stood across from the man, checking the tag of the receptacle. The tag had a moving picture of the man—pained expression, sorrowful eyes, mouth crying out for whatever these visages of humans cried out for. Within the image, the man wore a loose-fitting light blue hospital gown, and he laid flat on dirty white linen.

The visage within the tag called out again; though this time there was barely a whisper, "Robinette."

A suspicious Death peeled his eyes. *No.* The tags weren't supposed to have sound.

He put his ear to the tag, waiting for some confirmation that he hadn't just imagined some foreign speech.

Not a word.

He stood up straight, reviewing the tag further. The man still cried out, but soundlessly and in vain.

Death shook his head. How could he assess such an unexplainable moment? To analyze an imagined sound—such a divergent thought process was irrelevant to his work. The man in front of Death was his obligation, as insignificant as any one mortal was. Imagined noise or not, this was business as usual.

Looking back up at the being before him, the Pharmacist could see that the man matched the tag. His nose was more round than what might have been considered typical, and his mouth sunk back into his face. Hair receded far past the man's scalp and sat airily on his freckled head. Everything matched, except the expressivity shown in the picture. The human in front of him lacked all sentience, simply waiting for the dose of life essence that was never coming. The man was waiting for Death.

This one has met his end, Death thought to himself. *It is best that I get help for the gentleman.*

Tapping his hands against the smooth counter, Death willed such help into existence. Instantly, an identical being split from Death's body without diminishing the original's form. Now, there were two Deaths standing side by side. They were indistinguishable copies in every way, even sharing the same mind. This was omnipresence. With this power, Death could be everywhere within his pharmacy, all the time and all at once. Omnipresence had its uses for handling a never-ending line, and the ability also had the innate upside of allowing Death to think aloud at twice the speed.

He faced his copy, looking his own form up and down, examining every feature. Eyes appraised his tall body, dark-skinned, well-dressed in untainted white scrubs and an umbral lab coat that draped past his knees. He had sharp definition through his jawline, and his scalp lacked all hair, his skull neat and round. He took a wide stance, while his copy did the same. Then, he looked for any features that were similar to that of mortals.

Death always kept his thick lips straight, indicative of neither glee nor dismay. The humans in his line, the creatures who most closely resembled him, never showed the ability to shift their facial muscles with any profound exaggeration. Death understood why. What he didn't understand was why each tag showed sentient behaviour.

The original Death raised his hand to his jaw, tilting his head slightly. "The muscles around the cheeks, mouth, and eyes are communicative."

"Mortals have no use for them. They are frail dependent creatures," the copy replied as he gestured to the man. "The tags are a fallacy. These mortals only communicate their need for essence by looking longingly at the doses. So far as we've seen at least."

The original nodded to his other self, continuing his thought aloud, "Humans aside, what use do we have for these muscles? Yes, we are mild to an extreme, but that is simply the most efficient way to emote. Surely, we don't need to make the expressions shown in these pictures."

"These muscles are best used to maintain, not to express feeling. As it regards such expressivity, it is best to be a minimalist. Hence why the pictures are false. If these beings were sentient, they wouldn't be so suggestive. They would seek a status quo as we do."

"To be perfectly streamlined."

"And never over-extended."

Death felt the soothing wave of self-assurance wash over him. He knew his duty as the Pharmacist, and as he understood it, there was nothing else. He was the master cog in the machine that kept the balance between life and non-existence. He didn't need to worry about finding some indulgent purpose in his existence, or the existence of mortals. He was a mechanism of distribution, and that was enough.

Both Deaths looked back out, ignoring the man in front of them, insignificant as he was.

"Look at them, they aren't so aware."

"Certainly, they aren't aware of the planar split.

Whatever lay on the other side of that line is all that the mortals can be aware of. Only a fragment of their whole selves come to claim that which allows them to exist."

"Perhaps, they aren't even aware." This Death raised his left hand before his face and gripped it tightly, as though he was examining his own physical composition. "Our domain may be separate from the world of the living, but consider that it might just be the other side of a mirror. What if they were just as non-sentient and restrained on their side as they are on ours?"

Both Deaths raised their eyebrows at this, each returning the other's look.

"And they take their prescription just to live out their lives as zombified beings? Unaware and floating through time and space?"

The copy raised his head in contemplation. There was a long pause between the two Deaths, though it was broken when the copy answered with a question of his own: "Does it matter?"

Death had thought about that very question for as far back as he could remember. The lives of such beings surely wouldn't matter to the likes of him. He was the end and the beginning. He had his purpose. They, on the other hand, were all temporal gluttons. As far as Death knew, mortal lives were ones of indulgence, seeking only what he could provide for them. The pharmacy's purpose was that of crowd control, and the continuity of living creatures was within Death's authority. He kept the existence of sentient beings functional by dispensing to them their own lives. To do that efficiently, he needed perfect cleanliness in every aspect of his allotted plane. Clean scenery, sound, touch—all soothed Death as he worked.

7

The original returned his gaze to the man in front of him. *It is time to clean up the mess, isn't it?*

Suddenly, three copies of Death surrounded the man from all sides, and the empty figment of a human gazed upon the original. Death's sclera colored jet blue, and so did the man's in turn. Though completely entranced and void of almost all sentience, the human male's face appeared solemn. Death paid little attention to what he deemed to be an imagined sentience. He reached his right arm across the counter and placed his vibrant glove on the man's shoulder. Death looked deep into the man's soul where he bent the creature to his will. Now, the man would follow him freely.

The three copies took the man by his hands, and they led him across the threshold—the ebony counter becoming incorporeal as the duplicates crossed over. The original stood aside while the man was taken further into the pharmacy by the copies. Death watched his other selves open a pure white door to reveal a lightless path. While the door was open, the humming that always filled the air increased, and the darkness beyond the door slowly crept beyond the bordering doorway like an eerie infection of shadow.

When the door shut, the darkness shrunk back beyond the white door, leaving only the same bright light that always was.

Death closed his eyes to it for a moment. He was beyond the door and at the counter all at the same time. He was in one of a thousand rooms, strapping the man down to a black examination bed that stood alone in the middle of a speckless gray floor, far beyond the white door. Within a few seconds, the procedure was underway.

When the original returned his gaze to the line, his eyes were no longer that deep blue, and he continued his search for mortals.

The line picked up.

Deep blue life essence orbs appeared in the receptacles before being taken. The receptacles never moved, rather the tags changed to correspond with the next in line. Though each tag's image was a puzzle to Death, he had already decided against believing in such a colorful world of the living. He was stalwart.

Between conversations with himself, the maddening silence of non-sentient creatures was drowned out by the humming. Death tapped his foot at certain intervals, causing the most modest ruckus. In and of itself, the rhythmic hum was more vibration than sound, but it was the only noise Death knew to exist in his realm aside from his own voice and the clatter of his shoes. The audible variance helped fill the time as Death waited for an opportunity to recycle more life.

"This day's time is running short now," the duplicate began.

"I have a meeting soon," said the original. "It's with *that* person."

"I know. Who else is there?"

"No one. Though, I truly hate leaving the pharmacy for that very reason. I much prefer my own company to that of the Doctor."

Both Deaths nodded at each other in confirmation.

The original continued, "Maintain things while I am gone."

"Of course. I'll lead those without refills to the back. They will be taken care of."

"I know they will. We have never been anything less than perfectly efficient in herding mortals to the back. That's not what I'm worried about."

The copy raised his eyebrows again before speaking, "Do we worry?"

"No. I suppose we don't."

I have a few free moments left.

Death played to the silence one last time, letting the hum have one brief moment—collecting himself during the pause.

He returned his attention to his initial copy. "Do you know what we represent?"

The copy's voice was stern and crisp, "Order."

"Order," the original agreed. He raised his arm and stimulated his thumb against his index. "Order soothes the ears and eyes, and instills a sense of calm. It creates boundaries where the unknown doesn't threaten, and the unexpected cannot undermine. Consider that my line moves straight. No life-form is out of place. It is consistent, and when I am the end of one creature, another takes its place. That is the result of everything and everyone being right where they are meant to be." He snapped his hand closed and balled his fist mere inches from his face.

Both the copy and the original wore a slim measure of satisfaction on their faces—just the slightest simper. They spoke in tandem: "Beautiful."

The copy turned his attention back to the counter in place of the original, resting his hands against the sleek surface.

All the while, the original moved to the far right side of his pharmacy where a single door—half black and half white, separated vertically down the middle—created yet another threshold. This one was unique in that it was the only exit from Death's pharmacy.

He reached for the pure crystalline doorknob. *I do wonder... What marvel could there exist to rival my domain?* Death opened the door, and stepped into unyielding golden light.

CHAPTER **TWO**

The illumination beyond Death's pharmacy hit like a merciless haze, stinging the meat around Death's irises, forcing him to squint every time he crossed the black and white door. This golden hue was far more blunt than the bright whites that he was accustomed to, and it clung to him as he moved through it, thus changing the way his image resonated within space. It was as though his likeness was less sinister in this light—the aura forming around him creating a warmer exterior. Something about this place made everything soft, and Death was no exception. It neutralized everything that made him powerful and enigmatic. It took away his edge.

Disorder, Death thought to himself as he approached the tall spiral staircase that thrust up beyond what the naked eye could comprehend from its base. It had marble steps that mixed black, white, and gray in such a way that made Death cringe. There was a pearly railing on the left-hand side only.

This place lacks all symmetry and ignores what beauty subtlety would provide. He shook his head. *Just like her.*

Death took his first step upward, avoiding the railing out of spite. The clamor of his soles on the hard tread was a sound of which he neither disliked nor found pleasure in. Another step taken. And another...

The extensive climb was certainly felt by Death, and toward the middle he could peer down without seeing the black and white door—the airy golden ambience having obscured such long distances. Still, he pushed on, though he didn't really have a choice in the matter.

After reaching the top step, Death calmly ascended to a massive library, with bookshelves beyond counting, each one being several stories high. The shelves themselves were stained, pigments of brown and red glistening. The ceiling was a continuation of the same golden light with the entire mass swirling overhead at sluggish speed. Occasionally, the light overhead would form shapes—most often a detailed face with muted edges. Other times, the great golden fog was shaped like various creatures and people. The phenomena was curious, but Death had never allotted his time to solve its mystery. It was simply too superfluous a task.

The air around him smelled of ink and stale parchment, though he did his best to not breathe it in, or even to breathe at all. Such a choice was one of the perks of not being mortal. Breathing, after all, was utterly unnecessary. Still, he would catch glimpses of the scents, with the hanging fumes flowing into his nostrils as he walked on.

Wading through the stacks, he efficiently maneuvered

his way past shelved tomes and scrolls so plentiful that each single volume seemed redundant among the near-infinite collection; and that didn't account for the dozen copies that were made for those individual pieces. That thought occurred to Death at least once during each visit.

Getting lost in the stacks, just to find a book that says the same thing as twenty other texts... Once again, Death shook his head.

Of course, he knew his way through the maze of books, having been here for numerous other meetings. Regardless of the frequency of his visits, however, the library always gave him a sense of unease. It reminded Death that while he was powerful and omnipresent in his domain, he did not know all. The Doctor would always remind him of that: always, as in, for eternity.

The stacks opened up into a central domed foyer, where many persons clad in silver lab coats lounged in cushioned nooks, all of which were embellished with dozens of pillows and a disorderly sprawl of books. At the helm of the foyer sat a comely woman, who looked up at Death knowingly from her crystalline throne and smiled. This woman adorned a gold lab coat atop bright crimson scrubs. She was dainty with long legs and flawless ebony skin. Long locks of hair were interwoven to a single braid that flowed down past her ankles and draped onto gleaming marble at her feet. Death had always found the way her hair touched the floor to be appallingly unsanitary. Her auburn-eyed gaze was fierce—fiercer even than Death's. The Doctor, as she was known, pursed her bright red lips and shifted her eyes upon her contemporaries. Everyone retreated peacefully from their comfort stations upon being signaled, and in a matter of moments, only she and Death remained.

"You're right on time, my dear." the Doctor eyed the pharmacist, tilting her gold-rimmed glasses down just slightly.

"What you really mean is that you knew precisely when I would appear before you. That's why you planned the meeting for this time."

"Well, you're never late," she said, trailing off as she stood. She matched Death's height, nearing two meters, though despite her size, she moved more elegantly than the most graceful of creatures. With bare feet, she glided across the floor, and closer to Death.

"Well, you're never wrong." Death leered at the mess of books and pillows around him before continuing, "And yet, you still failed to send your flock away before my arrival."

"I thought you might enjoy seeing some lively faces for a change. Someone less gray. Really dear, you ought to get more help down at the pharmacy. All beings need company."

"I'm omnipresent. I keep my own company. You should know that."

The Doctor smiled, "I do indeed. It's one of the many things I know. I suppose knowledge is the greatest perk of being omniscient."

"You don't suppose." Death drew his hands tight, tensing his jaw. "Your use of imprecise language only serves to annoy me. Is that what you want?"

"No, that would be a waste of such a meeting. And we only scarcely see each other as it is..." She moved even closer, now just an arm's length from Death. "I simply want to catch up on current events. You and I, we maintain a great deal."

"We maintain everything really," Death added.

She chuckled at that. "If you say so, my dear. If you say so."

Death shook his head. He didn't want to hear about some omnipotent being that didn't truly exist. The Doctor just sought to rattle him, but he would not be unsettled by the likes of her.

"I assume I don't have to fill you in as it regards my operations," he remarked.

"Regarding your recent exploits..." The Doctor pointed up where light began to swirl overhead. The golden fog sharpened its dimensions, becoming more concise as it revealed a face. This was the face of the man that Death took prior to his meeting with the Doctor. This figment of the man showed the same expressivity as his image on the tag. The man called out, with no sound.

"You heard him, yes? You know, in that instance, he was calling for his daughter. His daughter, Robinette. In his last moments, he could feel the separation. Right before you touched him."

Death remained unfazed by the Doctor's ploy.

"I don't know what you have to gain by showing me this, but it is irrelevant. A single life means nothing. These humans may look like us, but they are simple beings. And I refuse to believe in something I have neither seen nor heard. So, hear me now. You may falsify images on tags and on your great ceiling, you may even have the tags make the occasional sound, but I will pay no mind to your endgame."

"Oh? Still stubborn as ever I see. The life of an old man is inconsequential to you, yes." She nodded to herself, maintaining her mischievous smile. "I should have known better."

"You know everything. You write the prescriptions for all life, and I fill them. Now what do you really want? Speak plainly for me."

The Doctor withdrew her smile.

After that, a hard silence was shared between the two, and neither showed any sign of retreat. It was always like this. She and Death had a symbiotic relationship, though they were often at odds with each other's methodology. One was tight and rigid, the other soft and loose. Yet, the pairing as a collective, and only as a collective, allowed for all manner of living beings to have their time on the other side of the planar split. Both understood the other's necessity, but their innate co-dependence irked each of them to no end.

"You know so little about humans. That much is clear. What do you know of their impact on the rest of the living world?" she asked.

"I told you to speak plainly, and you open with a jive and a question?" Death raised his eyebrows at his opposition, waiting for her to clarify.

There was no response.

"I've had enough of this." The Pharmacist turned quickly, and began walking back the way he came. He moved faster going than he had come, and was upon the edge of the foyer in no time.

"Wait," the Doctor called after him. "This is important. Crucial even."

Death paused. Ever-composed, he turned with grace, hands now behind his back. Casually, he made several steps back toward the Doctor.

"Death," she started, "It's time for a quell. The humans will have to have their numbers cut, for the sake of balancing all life. Therefore, I am going to redact several prescription lengths, and you will have to produce higher casualties."

Death thought about the decrepit old man who he had taken to the compound room just before leaving for this meeting. *Humans? Male.... Female.... Multi-faceted.... Infantile.... They are the same as all life.* He furrowed his brow at the Doctor. *Dependent on me, and my power.*

He nodded in agreement. "I suppose I can accommodate that."

"Do you suppose?" Despite the serious nature of their conversation, she still took a verbal shot at Death. The Doctor's openness was a mockery to the serious work that he actually accomplished, all the while she stayed in the background and came up with clever quips.

The Pharmacist ignored her and continued, "Still, there remains the issue of how to redact prescription lengths. I could allow you into my domain to alter what you have already set in motion, but I won't."

"You won't?"

"Stop it. You knew I wouldn't." He moved closer, reclaiming half the room as he stepped less than an arm's length from the Doctor. "I will personally redact the prescription lengths, given I have your permission. With your blessing, I can amend any failure of yours. That is balance."

She seemingly disregarded his last sentence, perhaps unable to reconcile Death's wording. Instead her next words focused on pushing her agenda, "That isn't ideal. I've looked at the possibilities, and I promise you..."

"I don't care what you know, or even what you think you know." Death stood tall. "It is my domain, and I alone hold power there. If you care so much about mediating the coexistence of all life, then you will abide by this condition."

The Doctor gritted her teeth and frowned, something that would make Death smile if he knew how.

"Do you know how infuriating you are? I have seen the possibilities!"

"Do I need to repeat myself? You know that I will." He tightened his hands behind his back and tilted his head knowingly toward her. "You've seen it already."

"There is an unspoken order of things. I write the prescriptions, and I alone can redact them."

"Unless I am given permissions, that is."

"Taking life freely is a dangerous gambit. You do understand this?"

"And what hands are more meticulous than mine? I am finely suited to the task."

The Doctor's red lips flared, fiery eyes beaming. She subtly bit the corner of her mouth before conceding. "A quell requires precision. That means managing the human's numbers effectively to a percent. We will cause more harm than good if we are careless, and that is a thin line to walk, I can assure you."

Death looked annoyed at the lecturous tone of the Doctor. "Again, with the redundancy. What is more precise than Death? Just give your permissions."

"Start with ten percent over ten days," she demanded. "Report back when that is done."

"That would involve me taking an additional one of every hundred humans." Death contemplated. "That's faster than I anticipated."

"Does that not suit you?"

Death stared at her plainly. "Those mortals are of no value to me. I have my purpose, and though it may involve their state of existence, I owe no being anything."

"And here I thought you were beginning to develop the ability to sympathize..."

"You thought no such thing," he shifted his feet and showed the Doctor his back. "You know I have no use for sympathy."

Death marched off, back into the unfathomable array of books. He thought while he walked, contemplating what had just occurred. *So, I am to take humans before their time.... I'll have to pick them at random too.* He loosened his hands behind his back, and came into his full stride. *With ease.*

Whatever the Doctor's reasons for quelling the humans was of no consequence to Death. Any would-be emotions for the creatures would complicate his job, and that was something he couldn't allow. He enjoyed the simplicity of just doing, and doing well. If that meant killing a tenth of humanity in a handful of days, then it would be done.

CHAPTER **THREE**

Death's pharmacy was booming, with hundreds of thousands of his duplicates roaming around the empty white plane to ensnare excess human life with the utmost efficiency. He counted out every 99 humans, and upon witnessing the 100th, he would create another copy to apprehend them. Fear became more prevalent on the faces of humans, and it wasn't long until Death began to wonder if his randomized approach had triggered some aspect of emotion from these creatures.

Their faces, he thought. *A fallacy. What awareness do they have? They cannot be so cognisant, otherwise they would feel gratitude. Without me, there would be absolute chaos. The line would be stagnant, and all life would feel its halt, regardless of their degree of consciousness. I treat them with a soft hand too, not that they would know it....*

The suspicion ate at him, but he chose to dismiss the possibility that these creatures could feel his presence. He had more pressing priorities anyway. If he failed to be efficient, then the Doctor would be justified in making a visit to his realm. He could not allow that. Her disorderly presence would only create greater opportunities for disaster. Besides, the only useful thing about her would be squandered here. The Doctor wouldn't be omniscient outside her own realm, just as he couldn't be omnipresent outside his. In the pharmacy, she would be nothing more than a self-righteous and indignant meddler. But then again, what could she hope to enforce without her power? How could she contend with Death?

He moved horizontally adjacent to the black counter, dragging his fingers across the very edge of its surface. His powdery blue gloves were more vibrant than usual, and his touch left a streak of residue. Immediately, Death created another copy of himself to deal with his own mess.

In the meantime, he observed the benefits of killing in excess. In the back of the pharmacy, the surplus amount of life taken was being recycled. Thousands of Death's copies were beyond the white door, moving through the surfaceless black plane and into more white doors—all thresholds radiating unevenly, fighting back against the darkness.

The mortals that Death claimed never fought being strapped down upon their final comfort: a black examination bed that sat next to a jar of brilliant cobalt powder. Unlike everything else in Death's domain, all of which was odorless, the rooms themselves had a scent of sterility. Antiseptic fumes came up from the rooms' gray floors and floated into a ceilingless space that ended with a far-off white light. There was a waist-high marble counter that ran the length of the nearside wall, and it served Death by offering him a surface to place his disposed gloves.

With a naked touch from Death's hands, all life ceased. He made a ritual of putting one of his dark hands over their eyes, and closing them. All the while, he let his other clenched fist hang over the massive jar. As said creatures began to shimmer and eventually blur, he released his hold on them, and they would seemingly evaporate. Nothing would remain of them on the black leather bed. When Death let his clenched fist unravel, the base for life essence sprinkled into the jar like celestial sand. This was the process for killing all beings.

The compounding rooms, as Death called them, were rarely visited by the original; and there was no one to object to his insistence of staying at the counter. He abhorred the pleasure he took in personally doing the behind-the-scenes business. At least with his duplicates, there was a degree of separation, albeit in his head. He felt and saw it all, but he could return to his place at the counter as he wished. Omnipresence always had some choice to it. While Death could never escape the knowledge of what his other selves did, he could ignore them and keep himself grounded.

He split himself again. This time his copy stood by him and examined the rate of cleansing. "Let's consider quelling a hundredth of the human population all in one stretch for today," he suggested to himself. "Then our duties would normalize until tomorrow."

The original didn't reply. Instead, he looked on and watched every hundredth human be marched to the back of the pharmacy. "A hundredth of today's population isn't the same as a hundredth of tomorrow's. Our number of redactions will need to be the same each day, for the duration. As you know, one of us is currently auditing the numbers. Once they are counted, we can deliver the appropriate amount of humans for the following nine days."

"The amount of life essence that we are recycling...It is tremendous. Perhaps a human prescription is worth more than most other life forms."

"An unexpected result," the original replied. "We will see a surplus for every life-form once this quell is finished." Both of them sighed in tandem. "I hate to admit that the Doctor was correct in instituting these randomized redactions."

"It is only because of her power. Not her innate wisdom. And she lords about on her crystal throne, giving permissions."

"Yes, that woman is not fit to bear the power of omniscience. Her knowledge of all things makes her a passable partner, in spite of her character. If we held that power..."

The copy picked up where the original left off, "Both sides of the planar split would see an unprecedented era of efficiency. Our gaze would know no horizons. We would be just shy of perfection."

Death, the original, walked past the counter and grabbed a field mouse from its place in the line. It stood in stasis atop the radiant blue material that covered his palm. He examined it, blue sclera mere inches from the minuscule beast, petting it gently as he took it back with him.

He glided as he returned to his copy's side. "Perfection can only be instituted by an entity who boasts omnipotence.

Since there is no evidence of such an entity existing, we make due by working alongside *that* woman." He held the mouse by its tail now, and placed it gently in his copy's hands. "I've dreamt of witnessing an act of perfection... As much as it would fulfill me to bear witness to an omnipotent being, or even some miracle that would expand my horizons, I cannot believe in what I cannot see. I alone hold these creatures with my hands. That's why I can only believe in myself."

The copy dismissed himself, and took the helpless field mouse to the back of the pharmacy. The original lingered. *What is it that I can't touch or feel? There is only life and me,* he thought to himself. His mind narrowed. *I am one half of everything, and yet, I am the only one striving to define what is perfect on either side of the planar split. The Doctor talks about balance, but there is no balance without me.* He gritted his teeth, cobalt pigment receding from his sclera. *She lets things become overgrown and forces me to fix them....*

It was at this time that the copy of Death that was designated for auditing the humans finished his job. The final selections were on their way to the back, and Death had an accurate number to eliminate during the next nine days.

Twenty five million. That was more than Death had expected, and it meant that there were well over two billion humans on the other side of the planar split. No wonder they needed quelling. Creatures always multiplied exponentially, Death knew that much. The more of them there were, the more would be created per the Doctor's grand plan.

Overpopulation really was her blunder.

All Deaths froze in place. The original whispered softly to himself, but it was understood across all his forms: "Twenty-five million will die consecutively tomorrow. The only randomization will be due to the order in which they come to me. I will relentlessly target the humans until my number is fulfilled." He exhaled cold air, a far more frigid realization setting in. "And then, while I still maintain the Doctor's official approval, I can enact a more drastic decline for this species. While I hold her consent, I have the power to do what I wish. She can't impede me without leaving her library and precious omniscience behind."

The thousands upon thousands of Deaths returned to their duties, while the original stood in silence. He felt a buzz on the inside of his chest, urging him to action. Death had never before wanted something this badly. Now that he held the power to redact prescriptions of life essence, he held the power to redefine the flow of existence and non-existence—not just for mankind, but for every species. And who better?

CHAPTER **FOUR**

The tenth day, Death thought to himself. *It's finally here. Over two hundred million of these creatures and my jars are beyond full. I'm creating more life essence than I am handing out. It's a boom.* Death furrowed his brow and let the edges of his mouth creep up so that his lips formed an awkward half-smile. *I can amend the number of jars easily. There is no concern for such things. Really, there are no concerns at all.*

The images of the senseless humans laying limp on his examination beds came to the foreground of his mind. Then his naked touch.

I will achieve the perfect efficiency for redistribution. If I hold a surplus, then there will never be too little to go around. The curve that his lips made managed to deepen in some areas while remaining the same in others. The half-smile was certainly lopsided, but it portrayed his enthusiasm enough.

During the past several days, Death's capacity for pleasure had expanded. Watching his jars fill with that bright blue powder at an unprecedented rate drew out something more than contentment. It was a joy to see the measure of his accomplishment, and he yearned for more. This initial quell of humankind was just the beginning— something to whet his appetite. Now, Death understood. The person who controlled the distribution of life essence controlled all beings. That type of power was simply insatiable.

While he felt this urge well up inside of him, he seemingly didn't care for the cosmic order of things— where the Doctor wrote the scripts and Death carried them out. Some part of him was left wanting a bit of disorder, so long as that disorder was managed by him and him alone. After all, he knew he could correct anything with this type of power.

Thousands of his copies were again ushering the humans back into the compounding rooms, but Death, the original, had spectated for long enough. He waded in the eternal white plane, long beyond his counter, at a point where he could experience the line up close. As the original, he wanted to see the line from a new angle, feel it out from a new perspective. And he wandered, the permissions awarded to him by the Doctor feeling untested so long as he delegated every kill to his copies. He had to take a life freely. It seemed the only way to really quench his thirst for extermination.

What is it like? He had almost forgotten the feeling. *It has been too long since I've killed without a degree of separation. Why bask in the experiences of my other selves when there is a pure intoxication to be had? I can do it indiscriminately now too. How can I pass that up?*

As the original Death, he just had to capture the feeling of siphoning life essence from a creature that had a pre-existing right to prolonged life. The desire for it had crept within his chest and nested there. He had to collect it for himself—some morsel of life for him to extinguish. Otherwise, what privilege did being the original yield?

What other creatures should suffer for humanity's decline? Surely they cannot go alone. That would create imbalance... He strode vigorously to the point where his pharmacy was merely a dot on the horizon. It was as though he was on the hunt, prowling the edge of his borders to claim some plethora of unexpecting creatures. He had no intention of sadism, nor did he bask in the supposed fear they wore when he greeted them. Rather, Death craved the feeling of killing painlessly the wayward souls that came to him. Nothing was as beautiful as the fade into non-existence.

Death walked past the various flora and fauna, unsure as to what might capture his fancy. The Pharmacist paused, tunneling his vision down the streak of grayed creatures.

In the distance, a single creature became apparent. This one was humanoid, but its place did not match the ebb and flow of Death's line.

What is this? He moved toward it. *Something is wrong.*

This divergent being was actually moving around as though it was sentient. Death began to pick up his pace, now to the point that he was almost running. Had the Doctor come down to inspect his work? How would she have gotten past him? He was everywhere!

A few steps closer, and he was second-guessing his interpretation of this creature. A few more, and he was entirely unconvinced that this was *that* woman or any of her people.

Unlike the Doctor, this dainty humanoid woman had straight golden hair and emerald eyes. Her skin was pink, a vast contrast to the bookish Doctor that Death had come to detest. A small turned-up nose gave her a gentle look. This woman wasn't overtly graceful nor was she large by what he had observed from creatures of her shape. She wore a brown skirt and a white top; no lab coat or scrubs. Her appearance differed too much from any person the Doctor kept, and Death had yet to smell the flagrant musk of self-righteousness that his counterpart and her brood excreted.

Who could this be?

Even stranger, the human didn't seem to fully comprehend where she was. Her sporadic movement implied that she could be exploring the pharmacy. This human was interrupting the flow of the line by examining the other beings, though perhaps the disruption wasn't intentional sabotage. All creatures had their place, but this meant that she would have created an empty spot somewhere among the hundreds of trillions of life forms. Would the other creatures fill it? Would the line halt completely? There was a real threat of unprecedented chaos invading his realm, and yet, Death was not trepid at the onset of impending disaster.

He was still.

Death couldn't help but stare at this anomaly who now wandered his plane. Disbelief was broadcasted through the hive-mind of his copies.

What manner of being encroaches on my domain without my foreknowledge? Death knew the answer as soon as he completed his thought: *There is none...*

His next step took conscious effort. And the next. And the one after that. There was a new sensation that crept across the surface of his skin and shook his frame. Death was drawn in by this human, but he felt more unnerved than ever. Interestingly enough, he knew this emotion from the faces of his victims; though it was now his dark skin that felt tight, his eyes welling with uncertainty.

Dread? No....Yes...? He shook his head. *How can I not know what I am feeling?*

As he strode close to her, the human stared at him in a way that no creature had done before. Those emerald eyes were more vibrant than the finest life essence he had ever produced, and they saw through him. Even as he loomed over her, she met him like an immovable object. She was absolutely fearless in the face of Death.

"Who are you?"

She boldly exclaimed, "I am Robinette."

Death stalled. He knew that name. It was the same name that the Doctor had mentioned when he had met with her last. Still, that explained very little, and he already resolved to not think of the humans he had already done away with. Regarding this woman though, Death didn't know of any being that was physically human, but acted with sentience. This Robinette demonstrated self-awareness by stating her name. But she was human, like that visage of the old man, calling out for this very woman without so much as a sound. Was this a trick set up by the Doctor? Or perhaps Death was meeting a new kind of human.

She kept her fierce look. Her voice was sweet and cool, "I was sent to die, wasn't I?"

The question was unexpected, and it created more uncertainties for Death to contend with. Part of him wanted to snatch all vigor and sentience from her and thrust her back into the line, while the other part of him pleaded to find answers to the desperate questions that plagued his conscience.

"You said you were sent... *Who* sent you?"

Robinette curled soft lips before chuckling softly. "Well, I can't be sure, but I assume it was God."

He traced her movements with his eyes. She bobbed her hips slightly and seemed to examine Death's reaction in the same way. A single drop of sweat trickled down his forehead—the tingle of perspiration being entirely new to the Pharmacist. He furrowed his brow and his dark eyes glazed over as he attempted to keep his cool.

"You know God, right?" She reached out and touched his bright blue gloves. "Right?"

He stayed visibly stunned.

Who is this God she claims to know? His mind began racing. *Surely it isn't me, and it wouldn't be the Doctor. Though that woman's flock treats her with reverence. I can't be certain.* Death looked down at where this woman held him. *Her touch....*

"Hello?" she raised her eyebrows expectantly. When she didn't get a response, her demeanor shifted. She hastily let go of his hands. "I can see that I've caught you off guard. It was not my intention. I just want to know who was sent to greet me."

Greet? Death was dumbfounded. "I'm....I'm supposed to kill you. Your kind is being quelled. Humans, that is... Right?"

"Quelled? As in being killed in mass?"

"I am Death. Killing is what I do."

She remained unmoving, blinking once slowly. Perhaps his statement had triggered something in her, or perhaps Robinette was simply indifferent to dying. Being a mortal, she probably felt the weight of impending non-existence, right? Death could only speculate, but he had always assumed that if mortals felt anything, they would feel the fear of no longer being alive.

How is she so unfazed by me? A mortal...

"You can't be left like this," said Robinette. "The state that you're in..."

Death found himself truly perplexed at that. In a half-hearted tone, he made his demand, "Explain yourself."

Rather than respond, Robinette reclaimed Death's hands.

Death shook his head, not fully keen to engage the woman physically. Though, he did manage a more able protest, "Whether you are mortal, or some higher power, I will have you know that this is my domain. You will explain yourself."

She pulled him closer.

Some unseen force overpowered Death's will to resist. He froze and began to unravel from within. Despite his nerves, he found himself getting towed in until he was so close that he could feel her breath on his neck. He focused on her. She remained steady, far more steady than him.

Suddenly, her free hand reached through the air and touched his brow.

What is she doing? Internal panic set in for Death. *I can't stop her. I'm powerless...*

"Easy now," her soft voice echoed. "I'm going to show

you much of what you've been missing. It's only right that you be given the chance to be more."

Her palm was smooth and it radiated warmth, the likes of which Death had never experienced. Robinette glided her fingertips to the edge of his eyelids, gently persuading them to close. Death had no choice but to embrace the darkness, and before he could comprehend what was happening, he, as the original, was solely detached from his copies.

Soon, his entire body felt new warmth, and some great radiant light touched the outside of his eyelids. When he opened his eyes, he had to wince to avoid the shock of such brightness. Death, the Pharmacist, was no longer in his domain.

CHAPTER **FIVE**

Death stood on a plane of green and brown flora, and as he adjusted his eyes, he began to search for something—anything that would constitute familiarity. The ceiling above him was softly blue and had shifting white plumes of what resembled fog. There was a powerful orb of light at the foremost elevation—some great height that Death couldn't comprehend. Every time he looked up to measure its distance, the surface of his eyes burned, and he was forced to retreat his gaze.

Keeping his head down, he stomped the uneven surface beneath him. His sleek black shoes roughed the green blades that reached for his ankles, digging into a soft collective of matter. Eventually, Death knelt down, and he found comfort in being small. He reached for his feet and sampled the ground with his massive hands. It was dark and cold, and it fell through his fingers like clumping dust.

Where am I? He brushed the remnants of grime on his

black lab coat in an attempt to cleanse his bright blue gloves. *The ground is malleable and filled with living things. Light comes from above rather than there being an ambience all around. Everything has color....every single thing.* He took an uncharacteristic breath. *Am I on the other side of the planar split? Or something else entirely?*

"It's clear that I'm not in my pharmacy," he muttered to himself. "But why can't I get back? What is the purpose of this journey?"

Death thought back to the way he froze upon being touched by Robinette. He had never permitted her such power over him, but somehow she had it. It was as though she had power in his domain, which was impossible.

"Am I in her world now? A place where her rules apply?"

Soft rustling grabbed his attention, and just the faintest whistle appeared from some unseen source. It touched him too, moving along his body as a pleasant compliment to the warmth against his skin. The force flapped the bottom of his umbral lab coat and curled his collar. Then, some fragrance touched his nose, and though it was raw, it was also sweet and refined. Perhaps the smell came from yellow and blue flowers, but how could he be certain? Surprisingly, the overload of sensations began to appease Death. The brisk air felt good on his skin now, and he was quickly acclimating to the scents bathing his inner nostrils. Eventually, he found himself drifting into a euphoric lull.

What puzzling sensations. He stared at the gloves he had defiled. *There is no cleanliness. No order.... And yet, I'm not entirely opposed to what I'm feeling.* He looked up again, shielding his eyes. *It feels nice, but I am yet to get my answers.*

Death moved under the wide spread limbs of a nearby tree. The shadows cooled him further and left his eyes thankful. He recognised the tree as a long-lived species of oak, the likes of which received life essence from him back at the Pharmacy.

Color. Life. Sentience.

"What does it mean?"

Just then, some manner of quaint laughter caught the Pharmacist's attention. It came from a nearby clearing just a dozen paces from Death's position. Three humans in modest but colorful dress danced on the grassy mound, running sporadically to grab the aromatic flora that spread across the ground. Two of them were young females and the other was male. The lot of them were scarcely taller than Death's waistline. Certainly, they were adolescents. The furthest most female had flowing auburn hair and a lime green dress that strapped over a blouse. Her face was pale with light red pigments that showed prominently on her cheeks. Her face was lightly speckled, especially across her nose, and her eyes were blue like the ceiling above. This girl remained close to the young male who emphatically spread his arms as he spun—his simple white shirt and brown pants flowing loosely on his undeveloped frame. He had a dark brow and an angular jaw. His eyes were a muddled green, and his nose was a bit larger than what Death would have considered to be proportionate to the rest of his face.

Death examined the scene further.

The other female had a bright blue dress and short straw-like blond hair. Her small up-turned nose made her look timid, but her stance was that of a young lioness. She flashed a smile while she twirled. A seemingly familiar set of emerald eyes glanced knowingly in Death's direction.

Robinette?

Death walked into the clearing. He loomed over the children awkwardly, but they didn't seem to mind. Instead, the three pink faces welcomed him with giggling, the likes of which Death couldn't comprehend. He didn't have time to ponder the curious displays before the young Robinette was beneath him.

"You took your sweet time," she said.

"You forgot the part where you explained how you did this to me," Death quipped back. "That's where we'll start. After that..."

Robinette grabbed his hand, and he was lulled once more—the same power she had utilized in his pharmacy overcoming him. "I'm sure it will be explained somewhere down the line, but for now, you'll have more fun if you just do what I do. This will be a lot easier if you just loosen up and follow my lead."

Robinette beamed up at him with excitement. "Just stay close to me. After all, I've been looking forward to this part."

Close to her, Death mentally reiterated. *Answers are close to her. And I am powerless....*

She led Death into the open area where the other two waited. No words were exchanged before the four of them formed a circle, outstretched arms connected, fingers firmly interlocked between each person.

Death meant to pause. He meant to excuse himself. He meant to ask what was happening, but before he could muster his voice, the four of them were running. They ran in a loop, with Death doing everything he could to not trip over his own excessively long feet. There was the rush of whatever cool invisible force it was that hit his face. The giggling grew to be boisterous, and all three young humans looked at each other with the same mischievous expression.

At this moment, Death looked over his shoulder at Robinette. He examined her from head to toe, not paying any mind to the increasing speed that the four of them were producing.

How is it that she is so small? How is it that everything has changed with her touch?

Before he could complete his thought, the children broke the circle and flew back into the grass. Death had no choice but to let the momentum take him as well, and he found himself on his back. Everything wobbled, and his head felt lopsided for a moment. So, he laid flat, and stared up at the swirling blue ceiling while he waited for his equilibrium to return. The blue above reminded him of life essence—the only pure and colorful thing that he had cherished. Now, he was on some plane of great color, dragged along by sentient beings. He felt like the consolidated white fog roaming overhead per some unseen force. He wondered if they too were dizzy.

Death knew this Robinette had done something to him when she closed his eyes. She must have. He imagined her unwavering stance and warm touch. That human surely had some type of power over him, though Death wasn't alarmed by it. Now, there was a miniature version of her, and that didn't alarm him either. Instead, curiosity ran over him.

I know it's strange, Death thought to himself. *Of all the questions that I need answered....I mostly want to know who she is.* There was a bit of an internal conflict there though. *Am I not Death, who has killed countless beings? Why am I forced to be led around by mortals?*

More giggling came from down the slope, this time with intermittent and high-pitched shrieks. Death sat up and saw the girl in green and her male counterpart rushing down into heavy tree cover. Standing beside the Pharmacist was the child Robinette, eyes glittering in the golden light. She offered her petite hands and urged him up before letting her touch fade.

"Come on," she said, her voice soft and pitched.

"Wait," Death called out to her.

Instead of answering, she ran into the trees after the others. What choice did Death have but to follow?

The young Robinette raised her knees intermittently and hopped as she ran. It was a motion Death would never have considered viable—especially considering his lanky frame, and yet, these humans tramped around playfully. They were utterly without definite time constraints, and they weren't compulsively adherent to efficiency. Still, no matter how strange it felt, Death lumbered through the woods with the hopes of discovering the meaning of their acts.

Down into the darkened woodlands, the four of them came to the edge of some glistening stream that coursed through the ground and trickled over stone—pieces more coarse than his counter, and resembling marble if it was broken into variably sharp fragments. Death halted at a soggy border where his shoes slipped into the ground. He took in everything around him. There was a pool that showed no bottom, and it was calm save for some ripples. Upslope and to Death's left, the fluid substance crashed down and dispersed amongst itself, thus creating white reflective foam. Life also teemed in this area, with small beasts roaming the trees and fish and amphibians being present in and around the stream.

The three humans rushed into the stream, each of them letting out gasps as their legs and waists were quickly submerged. The young male found the reactions of his contemporaries to be especially amusing, and began to grasp the stream and pitch it at the others. Pandemonium ensued and the trio began to engage each other with indiscriminate splashing. This volume displacement that came from their movement created a unique sound that merged with subsequent laughter. The humans were all smiles and wide eyes. And then, in the midst of their splendor, they turned to Death, who looked back at them oddly.

Cold liquid burst from their hands and soaked the Pharmacist. He shriveled and took several quick breaths. His arms were folded tight against his ribs, shoulders bending forward and making him small. While the tall figure was stunned, the humans grabbed him by his black lab coat and dragged him into the middle of the pool.

"Ohhhh...." Death's lips vibrated. Liquid filled his shoes and scrubs.

The young people surrounded him. For whatever reason, Robinette's peers failed to see him as a stranger. It was as though they were preoccupied by the moment, finding amusement with Death's shivering and trepidation.

"Come on," Robinette said. "Don't just stand there."

They splashed him a few more times, with the cold causing Death to reel. The Pharmacist instinctively splashed back in a desperate attempt to reclaim his own space, and in doing so became the center of the chaos. Eventually, the exhilaration overtook him, and his face began to stretch in new ways—a more pronounced and crooked smile with cheekbones high and teeth showing awkwardly.

These humans...they look at me happily. He couldn't imagine the humans he knew from his pharmacy looking at him in such a way. Even the images on the tags showed fear and pain. Somehow this was different. Clearly, he wasn't in his domain anymore, but he could have never expected this. There was no threshold that separated existence and non-existence here. There was no order. No existential duties outside of the innate responsibility to oneself.

Death closed his eyes instinctively as a quickly thrown torrent caught the side of his face. He arched into the stream and rushed forward with all of his might, creating a wave that toppled the young male. He whipped his arms across the surface and sent another splash at the other two. His baritone laughter boomed as he took the center of the stream. The display of emotion was more surprising to him than it was for the small humans. They just kept enjoying themselves. They kept enjoying his company, and he did the same.

I am Death. He thought as he splashed and dunked the children. He was utterly immersed in the act at this point. *I am endless. Unconquerable. Unforgiving.*

After what seemed like hours, Death found himself on the bank, and laid defeated. He was tired, the likes of which he had never felt.

Robinette drew within arm's length of the Pharmacist, standing over him. His smile faded as the others abruptly stilled in the stream. The ambience of droplets now dominated in the absence of laughter. All eyes were on Death and the young girl.

"It's time," she said.

Time for what? Death felt the weight of extreme awkwardness. *Why the sudden pause? Is this not proper human behavior?*

The Pharmacist scanned the others to gain some hint as to what he did wrong. The young male stood with the long sleeves at his sides dripping back into the stream. The girl with auburn hair dropped her head a bit. The two of them waved to him in tandem, with neither of them expressing the same joy that they had all shared just moments before. Death knew that their waving was a communicative gesture, but he couldn't guess what it meant.

He turned back to the girl with emerald eyes, Robinette. She was steady and never dismissed the knowing look from her rosy face. She maintained her smile.

He reminded himself: *She has the answer.*

Every bit of this experience so far had felt surreal, and yet he had gone along with it. So, when she reached out with her hand, he lowered his face to meet her touch. The soft unblemished hands of youth gently brushing down his brow signified a transition. Death closed his eyes again.

CHAPTER **SIX**

The Pharmacist found himself in a massive room that was equally tall and wide. Three stories up, the ceiling was adorned with silver chandeliers, all of which were bedazzled with dangling jewels. Each fixture provided a crisp yellow hue that extended its light proportionally across the grand hall. Romanticised paintings hung on white walls, and their grandiose depictions seemed to fit the ambience of the space—robust colors alluding to the depth of such fantastical scenery. Swarms of finely dressed humans stopped at the edges of the room to look at the paintings, where they whispered well-practiced critiques among themselves.

At the center of the floor, the grooveless mosaic tiles were often covered by pairs of people who embraced each other. These pairs moved as one, and glided to different portions of the room, all seemingly swayed by the sweet thrums and well-timed scores that now enticed Death's ears. They were seemingly apart from other humans who sat at tables or lined up along the back wall where men in white uniforms distributed some manner of aromatic matter that was put on display.

The group in the back reminded Death of his line, though these humans were clearly more active. Still, they filed orderly and yearned for what was supplied. At least that aspect of human behavior was familiar. Perhaps the matter was nutritional based on how the humans sought to consume it. Death couldn't figure what it was made of though. Everything in this place was entirely foreign after all.

This is unnerving. I'm not accustomed to being in crowds of people. Not actual functioning people. He looked around, hoping to find that one familiar face.

Death felt a tap on his shoulder, causing him to turn quickly. Robinette stood beside him now, and she wore a flowing blue dress accoutered with tasteful lace across her sternum. The dress itself accentuated her most womanly features. It was clear that she was no longer an adolescent, though predictably, Death still towered over her. Her yellow hair was tied up, and there was enough volume to imply a greater length than she had displayed at any point before. She pursed her lips, raising a single eyebrow.

"You," Death managed.

"Who else?" Robinette chuckled softly. Smiling, she held out her hands—long white gloves running the length of her bantam forearm. "Shall we?"

Death looked at her puzzled. "Shall we...what?"

"Oh, come on." She pulled Death out to the center of the room where others whirled to mellifluous sound. She looked at him sternly. "Grab my waist."

"Your waist?"

Robinette sighed. She grabbed his hands and placed them in the appropriate positions. This way, she was so close that Death could smell her floral scent, and it was akin to the fragrance of the blue and yellow flowers of the grassy knoll where he had met her younger self.

"Just follow me," she demanded. "And don't step on my feet."

In mere moments, Death was being swept across the room, his firm-heeled shoes clattering on the sleek floor. As he moved, the melodies seemed to vibrate the air around him and affect the tempo of his motions. In his head, Death focused solely on not disrupting his partner's lead. To do so would be to incite chaos, and Death didn't want chaos right now. He wanted to follow her.

She leaned in and whispered in his ear, "You're better than I expected. Do you dance on your side much?"

"No, I just recognise the order that you are enforcing with each movement. I know something of order."

"So, killing brings order?" The question had a weight that Death hadn't anticipated.

"More precisely, killing brings balance." Death stuttered in his stride briefly, but used his long legs to recover swiftly. "I bring order."

"That's a bold statement."

Death stared into her glowing green eyes. When Robinette did the same, he averted his eyes. The quick change made him stumble, and she was forced to catch him.

"Perhaps too bold," she said as she helped straighten Death.

"You mortals wouldn't understand."

She lowered her eyes. "Oh?"

"I determine what exists and ceases to exist. In my domain, I am ever-present. My very touch can turn a creature into dust."

"Your touch doesn't seem to be so lethal now," she smiled knowingly.

Death peered at his long hands, one wrapped around her petite waist while the other enveloped her hand. "It's the gloves," he exclaimed. "They are a barrier. If I gave you my bare touch, you would break down into life essence. You would crumble in my grasp and fall through the cracks of my hands."

"That's all very exciting," she said half-heartedly.

"It is."

"So, is Death painful?"

The Pharmacist shook his head. "Death is my name. As to whether or not I am painful, well, I have no way of knowing." He gulped, tensing his shoulders and looking away. "I do my best to be gentle, but there is a thrill. I'm not sadistic, but..."

"But you long for touch," she finished. "Maybe it makes you feel closer to the living. Less alone. Something like that, right?"

Death furrowed his brow at that. Her conclusion was a curious one. It was something he hadn't considered, and until this moment, he would have dismissed it as folly. Yet something about that claim felt alarmingly accurate.

How does she speak as though she knows? Even the Doctor doesn't read me so well, or at least not so sincerely. Death felt a new heat appear beneath the skin of his cheeks. *She is special. Somehow. This human is special.*

"You're flushed." Robinette laughed. She tightened her

grip on his hands so he couldn't pull away.

Death knew what she was alluding to: some automatic physical response that conveyed excitement or nervousness. He wouldn't have it. He was Death. He couldn't have it. The Pharmacist ground his teeth and gave a deep exhale through his nose. None of these actions alleviated his display of embarrassment. Death felt his face grow even hotter.

"What has gotten you so red?"

Death had no choice but to blatantly deny any such reaction.

"I don't get flushed. That must be a mortal thing." He shifted his eyes from her steady gaze, hiding them under his dark brow.

Robinette ignored his counterfeit claim completely. "It's okay. I was just curious as to what you were thinking about. A being of your caliber doesn't often get flustered, I'm sure. So, you must have had quite the thought."

The sounds slowed in tempo, and as a pair, Death and Robinette began to move more gently. This gave Death the perfect opportunity to change the topic: "What is all this? The sounds. The clothes. Everything. What purpose does it have?"

Robinette raised an eyebrow. She moved her eyes without tilting her head, seemingly scanning the room. "All of this pageantry you mean?" She refocused her eyes on him. "It is supposed to be a joyful event. People don their best attire, assert their status with pride, eat like royalty. Mostly, it is a coming of age. People like me are supposed to celebrate their best years."

"That sounds feasible if it is indeed the purpose of humans to experience joy. It is quite...What's the word?"

Robinette completed his thought, "Vain."

"So vanity is the purpose of humans?"

She shook her head. "Maybe for some, but purpose is relative for us humans. Generally, at least." Robinette leaned in, her chin just shy of touching Death's collar. She whispered, "You see, being human is about learning what your purpose really is. It isn't innate. It isn't written on the fiber of your being. It lingers as a big question until you've chased answers for so long that you've established a lifetime. And if you are lucky, you would have established a beautiful and full lifetime."

As he embraced Robinette, Death let her words sink in. *A human's purpose is finding said purpose? Why isn't that absurd to me?* He thought of all the humans he had killed. They were beyond counting. Were all of them searching for purpose on their side of the planar split? What if he had taken them too soon? That would mean one thing.

Death's eyes went wide. *Disorder.*

"Oh?" Robinette smirked. "Another big thought huh?"

"I suppose." He narrowed in on her swirling green eyes. He spoke truly, "Yes. Yes, indeed."

She spoke forwardly, "Tell me about it."

"Well, I was just wondering about sudden non-existence for such creatures as yourself. If you are actively seeking purpose, then what happens if you are killed before finding it?"

"I can't really answer that." Robinette seemed to hold back for just a moment. "That question is bigger than me."

"No," Death replied. "You have answers."

"I have experiences to share. That much is true." Her lips curled, almost as though she was considering how to explain something inexplicable. "I can't fully tell you all the hows and whys of what is transpiring between us. It's just happening. I saw you and I knew that I couldn't leave you there in that blank space of a world. I couldn't let you live a shell of a life, with nothing to fill the void."

"What void?" He asked. "I don't live to begin with. I merely exist!"

"I suspect that is the problem."

He looked down on her. "Tell me more."

"I only know so much, really. I can only guess that the existential questions will be answered later on. I can show you what value human life has through the lens of my life, but that is the extent of my part in all of this." She laughed nervously. "It must be so complicated. It's so much bigger than we know, isn't it?"

Yes, Death thought to himself. *It is complicated. At least it seems to be.*

Death danced on without pressing for answers. He felt a new sensation curling in the pit of his stomach: Doubt. Not everything was as it seemed from his side of the planar split. These revelations were leading to something, but he was neither omniscient nor versed in whatever cosmic workings had overtaken him and this woman.

Robinette stopped moving. The other humans continued to circulate around the two of them. She looked up at Death and motioned to the far wall, "Look up there."

There was an overlooking balcony peeking out from the second floor. It was without any occupants, overlooking the dance floor where the masses had gathered. Its railing was shaped gray stone that had some curvature to it, and beyond was something like a curtained double door.

"Make your way up there, and I'll bring you some food."

"Food?"

"Trust me." Robinette smiled as she parted from him.

~~~~

Death stood on the balcony where he leaned over the railing, the long sleeves of his black lab coat crumpled against the carved stone. He watched the humans from above. Most of them looked uncomfortable in their own skin, while others were overly theatrical. Robinette had said that these gatherings were for enjoyment, but there seemed to be hidden social obligations.

And where does she fit in here? Death looked down at Robinette who stood at the front of the line next to the table with serving men. Those men in white clearly served those dressed in finery, but perhaps they took something in return—much like Death did when he led living beings to the compounding rooms. Though, interestingly enough, no one was ushered away by these men. Could it be that they really were just servants?

Is there equality among their ranks? Death considered Robinette's recent words about human purpose. *Could that even be possible if each person is actively searching for their purpose? Would that not breed competition, or even conflict?*

At this time, Robinette made her way up the stone steps and to the balcony where Death resided. She held two discs, both of them a muted gray metal, and atop of them was an array of aromatic treasures. She handed him one of these discs along with a pronged metal tool.

Death looked down at the green leafy substance, and starch wedges. There was a bone with steaming red chunks on it as well, and a gold-crusted slice of white spongy matter sat on the edge of the dish. The Pharmacist really didn't know what he was supposed to do with all of it, but the smell enticed him nonetheless.

"I come up here to eat because I don't coddle my food like many other ladies." She nodded down to the well-dressed women sitting at tables, before shoveling a scoop of greens into her mouth. She continued speaking despite her mouth being full, "Go on then."

Death followed Robinette's lead by putting the food in his mouth. He was quick to discover how it made his mouth water, and that his sense of taste was instantly immersed in the food's flavor. He moved his jaw so that his teeth ground the flavor down before swallowing. In all manners of speaking, his form for chewing was probably atrocious compared to the humans. His mouth had solely been a means for projecting his voice until this point.

He looked over at Robinette, who chewed a mouthful—up, down, and side to side. By her own admission, she wasn't the most graceful either.

"So," Death started with his mouth full, "the purpose of food is pleasure?"

Robinette choked down her last bite before laughing. "No," she exclaimed, "it's sustenance. We humans get hungry as we move around and burn energy. Dancing is especially good for that."

The Pharmacist nodded while taking another bite. "And where do you get this nutritious matter from?"

"Plants and animals."

A wide-eyed Death stopped chewing all together, spitting out his food back onto the metal disk. He quickly set it down on the ground, and emphatically looked for something to wash his mouth with.

How could I ingest their parts!? He thought about every type of creature and plant that moved through his line. Their glazed expressions and limp bodies came to mind. *Unclean! Unclean!*

Robinette handed him a glass of red liquid. "Drink this to calm your nerves."

Death did so, and in a large way, too. After several gulps, he instantly regretted the dry bitter taste. Still, there was no way plants and animals could be turned into liquid. At least, that assumption was a comfort to him.

He took a breath, "Why would you ever consume other beings? Can't you get nutrition from other things? Something that doesn't stand in my line?" He paused for a second. "Like stone! You could consume stone! It would be so much cleaner."

Robinette's face curled, and she held her free hand over a wide grin. She lurched and had to set her own disk of food down.

She swallowed before speaking, "Outrageous!" Remnants of her chuckling rippled through the air. "That's just not how the world works. All living beings have to consume other living beings to replenish their energy." She paused to think. "Well, I suppose plants don't. I think they convert sunlight."

Death stood there stunned. Had he been killing flora and fauna so that other creatures could consume them? That was madness.

"I can tell that the thought distresses you," she said.

"You told me to trust you!"

Robinette held up her hands, still smiling. "If anything, it's a good learning experience. Just take a deep breath."

Death did as she said. He felt his initial anxiety begin to diminish. Suddenly, he began to feel some of the effects of that liquid too.

"Maybe that was just too in-depth for you. I thought you might admire the balance of our ecosystem, being as obsessed with order as you are." She lowered her hands. "It's all right now though."

Order...yes. Okay. Death took another hard breath. Part of him wanted to laugh, while the other part of him was still stupefied.

"It's curious," she suddenly changed topics. "Eating aside, I hadn't considered it before."

"What is that?" He looked at her, hoping she wouldn't spring any more surprises on him.

"I bet this is the first time that you are such an outlier, huh? I looked around your line, and there is no one to bring contrast to your life. In your pharmacy, you are only surrounded by yourself."

Death stood silent.

Robinette looked out among the crowd. "I've been different my whole life, you know. I might have considered how much of a culture shock you would experience."

"You are different?" Death looked out at the other humans. "You look the same."

Robinette gave him a knowing look, and Death reeled a bit.

Right. You were sent to me.

"I've never really enjoyed all of this finery. My purpose is somewhere else. Something bigger. Do you know what I mean?"

Death nodded, not knowing what to say to that.

She sighed, seemingly pondering something personal.

Eventually, she lightened up, and spoke, "It's about time, don't you agree?"

"Time for what?"

She reached for his eyes. "It's time to move on from this drab party, and experience something that I know you will enjoy."

CHAPTER **SEVEN**

Death was welcomed by cold air and a lightless room. He bumped his head against an overhanging beam that was hidden in the darkness, causing him to lurch back a few steps—his hard heels rattling the hardwood floor below him. The vague shapes around him seemed to blur as he squinted his eyes, and tensed the point of his forehead where he was struck.

Where has she taken me now? He clenched his teeth, regaining his vision, and doing his best to not stumble in the dark.

There was a flicker, and the sound of small-scale friction alerted his ears to a point in the room where a growing red and yellow glow began to illuminate the area. Robinette stood there, holding a lantern at shoulder height. She had what must have been a white nightgown on, with wool trousers and a coat over it. She held thick linen under her free arm, and brought a finger to the tip of her thin lips.

She whispered, "Quiet while we're inside, okay? Humans sleep at this time of night."

Death gave her a confused expression.

"We won't be in here long." Robinette moved past him, but not before offering him a mischievous smile. She meandered to the far side of the room where there were large double doors that were mostly thick glass at their center. The doors were covered by thick blue drapes that blacked out whatever light was beyond. "Come on, let's not dawdle. I have a surprise for you."

She opened the door, and revealed an all-white Victorian balcony that looked out over the seemingly endless dusk. Cold air swept through the doorway and swam across the surface of Death's skin. It was at this time that he cursed his scrubs for being made of thin pliant fabric, as it left him unprepared for the chill of the human world.

Robinette stepped out onto the balcony and beckoned Death to follow. The Pharmacist complied, and when he emerged onto the platform, he viewed a new ceiling— endless dusk that was pierced by shining twinkles of white light. These twinkling spectres seemed to burn, though they did so from a great distance, thus the perception that they were small. In this way, the overcast seemed less like a ceiling and more like an expanse of unending dark space that was suspended above Death.

The sound of the door closing behind him alerted Death to Robinette at his side. He responded by reclaiming his jaw from the meat of his neck and resealing his thick lips.

"I told you it was a surprise." Robinette raised a single

eyebrow and offered a closed-mouth grin. She thrust the lantern toward a stunned Death. "Hold this for me."

He grabbed it and held it at length from his face, meanwhile Robinette moved to the edge of the balcony railing, its thick round guard firm against the small of her back. She peered up at an overhang that came within an arm's reach of her head and seemed to study it for a moment. Then, she threw the linen up, freeing her hands. And with great agility, Robinette climbed onto the railing. Death lurched forward instinctively, but she waved him aside while she claimed her balance. Suddenly, the bulk of her weight was firm against the overhang, and she muscled her way to its top surface; and Death no longer had sight of her.

"Death!" Robinette's hand was suddenly in view. "Hand me the lantern."

"What?"

Her hand shook impatiently. "Give me the lantern. You can't climb up with it."

"Climb?"

"Of course. The view is best up here. I'll help you up, okay?"

Easy for a hand to say. Death thought to himself. He couldn't see Robinette's face, but somehow he imagined her rolling her eyes at him and wafting an unseen hand impatiently. The thought was as cringe-worthy as it was likely.

She called down again, "I will make you stay on that balcony for all time, never moving on from this scene of my life. You need to get up here now!"

What an infuriating mortal, but also... He raised his eyebrows and thought about the type of person who would demand from Death himself. *She has this spark. It doesn't wane in the face of risk or even a killer like me.* His crooked smile was likely wicked-seeming on his face, though he truly meant for it to be soft. Then, he stepped forward.

Moving to the edge of the balcony, Death forced a measuring glance over the railing. The drop was several times his own height at least, and he contemplated what would happen to him if he took that fall. It wasn't as though he, as an entity, was killable—at least not through physical harm. As far as Death knew, there would always be a version of him on his side of the planar split, and that came with being omnipresent. Even if his original body faded, his oldest copy would just take his place and continue the duty of killing and dispensing to mortals. So what was the risk of braving the slick ledge before him?

"Hey!" Robinette held out her hand expectantly, and Death obliged her implied request by lifting the lantern to where she could reach it. Her eyes sparkled at the moment of exchange, with the yellow and red lantern glow making the greens in her irises appear molten. She nodded past him and toward the railing.

"Yes, Robinette. I will comply, and should you keep me trapped within this plane of existence, neglecting to touch my eyes, then I will grant you a touch of my own." He meant for his threat to be playful, but also deterring. He didn't look back to see how she took it, rather he reached his long legs onto the beveled railing and drew himself up. He balanced for a moment and shifted his feet. After a while, he refaced Robinette, and attempted to shape his face to imply the whimsy he had discovered so recently in the stream. "You don't want to turn to compound and get lost in one of my jars."

She raised a single eyebrow and spoke, "If you threaten me again, I'll push you." The statement was deterring enough now that Death was up on the ledge.

He swallowed his smile as he stood tall on the railing, his lower diaphragm now level with the overhang. His slick black shoes had just enough of an arch in the soles to rock from heel to toe on the railing edge, though Death righted himself by grabbing hold of a corrugated gutter that made up the roof's foremost edge. Then, he exploded off the railing, in the same way that Robinette had done, and his upper body met coarse shingles in the process. His scrubs ripped slightly at the point of friction as he wriggled his legs into place. The Pharmacist let out a gasp, with fingers clawing at the down sloped surface. Robinette grabbed him under the arms, and with surprising strength, assisted him in finding his back.

"See?" She let out a hard breath. "That wasn't so hard."

She grabbed the linen and laid beside him now, offering him a knitted white blanket that boasted frayed edges from frequent use. Death took it, and watched as she enveloped herself with a similar blue cover. He mimicked her action by covering his torso and shifting his back against the coarse shingles until he found a comfortable position. He kept his legs bent with both feet bracing against the slight downslope as he maneuvered under the cover. He hugged his arms together and shimmied the blanket up his shoulders. All the while shivering, Death was relieved that the blanket deflected the cold air now.

"I gave you the warmer one. I figured you'd be less acclimated to the night air."

"Night?" He looked up. "Is that why the ceiling has darkened?"

Robinette gave a faint smile. "Good observation." She pointed up, seemingly at nothing in particular. "The sky is an endless ceiling that changes with the light of the sun."

"And what is the sun?"

"A star. It yields all light and heat known to humans. It is impossibly large, but extremely far away."

"So it is farther away than usual during the night?"

"Not quite." Her finger moved to a massive glowing stone far overhead. The stone was pale but illuminate, and it was so big that Death could see blemishes on its surface despite it being incomprehensibly far away. "Just there, the moon is shining while the rest of the sky is dark. That means we are facing away from the sun and that its light is reflecting off that giant rock. In the morning, we will face the sun again."

"I think I can understand the need for both light and dark."

"It's not just light and dark." Robinette looked over at him and they locked eyes. "Consider that you aren't the only thing that brings balance between the living and the deceased. Warmth, cold. Light and darkness. Awake, asleep. Living and dead. Love and the absence of love. Maybe it takes more than just you to manage all of that."

Death gave a contemplative nod, somehow finding her challenge of his worldview refreshing. *Is it unusual to feel so close to a living being? Somehow, I appreciate her by my side. It's like I want her to be my equal.*

Robinette pointed to one of the glimmers in the sky. "Do you know what those are?"

"No, I don't."

"They are stars, beaming light from the heavens beyond the sky. Each one of them is a sun, like the one whose light is keeping you from freezing right now."

Death replied plainly, "But I am cold."

Robinette chuckled and she scooted closer to him. She placed her head next to his shoulder, and Death had to fight off the urge to go rigid, new warmth running through his veins and to his chest.

His nerves ran wild, and his thoughts sped: *Why do I want her to be present even when I can't keep my body in check because she is next to me? That's not order. I'm enticed to take on vulnerabilities I can't fully pinpoint. At least, they feel like vulnerabilities.*

She continued looking up with a dreamy gaze. "Just look. Look up and imagine how large the universe is."

Death did as she said and found himself mesmerized. Then he thought about the infinite white space that surrounded his own plane of existence. It went on forever as far as he knew, much like the stars in the heavens.

"I can't tell you about all the wonders that are hiding out of our reach, but I dream about them often. I have all my life."

"Dream?"

"Not so different from what you're doing now I suppose. You're imagining, contemplating, exploring the unknown with your mind, right?"

Death nodded.

"Dreaming is just doing that when you aren't conscious."

"So dreaming gives you knowledge?"

A quaint laugh vibrated off of Robinette's thin lips. "With how much I dream, and how vivid they come... I'd know everything if that was the case."

"I know one person who knows everything." He

turned to her. "Really, she is omniscient. And despite her gift, she is insufferable. I couldn't imagine looking up at the stars with her. She would just antagonize me and attempt to assert dominance. Even as a human, you make much better company."

"Even as a human?"

"Well," Death paused. He searched for a soft reprieve to pair with his last statement, but he found no such follow-up.

She spoke matter-of-factly, but without any harshness, "It may sound strange to you, but despite being small among infinite heavens, I feel comforted. I feel comforted because there are people, just as inconsequential as me, keeping each other company. We give each other meaning, and we give each other love. And I will take that over knowing everything there is to know. I'm glad to be human."

But you are different, Death thought to himself. *Where is there room for contentment? Even an anomaly like you is just a pawn.* He couldn't understand how she could be content without some measure of control. Both the Doctor and himself dictated the state of her existence. And even if there was more out there, with the heavens and the stars and a "God"—that just meant that there was more controlling her, right?

Is being human really a good place to be in the order of all existence? Death dropped his chin and furrowed his eyebrows. His eyes wandered toward Robinette.

"Did you ever dream of the pharmacy? Of me?"

The left corner of her lips raised, forcing her cheekbone to round. Her eyebrows slanted as though she had just picked up on something. "Waking up in your pharmacy, it was like I was in one of my dreams. Everything fell into place after I laid eyes on you. I knew what to do, where to take you."

Death gave her a stern look. "That doesn't answer my question."

"I know. I can't really explain it."

He had no choice but to accept that.

"There is a lot, Death. This experience must feel very compact for you. Rushed. Forced." Robinette took another glance at the stars and stretched her arms. "We can just lay here for a while and forget the journey for the time being. I can close your eyes for you after I teach you the names of the constellations."

Death tightened his body beneath his blanket, and prepared for however long night was supposed to last. Truly, he hoped it would be lengthy.

CHAPTER **EIGHT**

Death found himself in a dusty room that was crowded with dozens of wooden boxes. White walls were largely neglected, all peeling paint and splintered surfaces. The ceiling wasn't high at all—not compared to most rooms that Death had experienced, but at least he hadn't hit his head. That said, he could have certainly done without the stale air lingering in his nose and lungs. It was as though life hadn't thrived in this place for a long while. There were brown curtains on the far side of the room that hid the area from sunlight even. Only small tidbits of natural light trickled in. There was a low flame within a large black wood stove at the back wall, which boasted a wide pipe that ran up through the ceiling and into the second floor. The overall state of the room was enough to make Death cringe.

He stepped and the hardwood floor moaned beneath him. Death examined the extent of the space, and it seemed a wide room with two windows, a door in front, and some stairs on the right. There were a few end tables with what looked like lamps underneath sheets of linen. A single lacquered rocking chair sat in the corner of the room, its wood being the only well-kept surface that Death could find.

This is a significant change of scenery, Death thought to himself as he strode to the middle of the room. *So unclean...*

The Pharmacist looked in the boxes and found various trinkets and decor items. These items were in pristine condition compared to the rest of the place, and the lack of dust made it seem as though they were recently brought in. Delving further, Death found some of the discs that humans ate food off of—these were glass, not metal. Utensils were buried as well. In other boxes, he found books, an empty lantern, more linen.

What to make of this...

Light footsteps were betrayed by creaky stairs behind the far side wall. Robinette emerged from around the corner. She wore a glowing smile and her clothes had their usual vibrancy. White stockings were matched with a bright yellow dress, and her feet were covered by black flat-heeled slippers. Her wispy blonde hair laid steady beneath a lace bonnet.

"I thought I heard you down here perusing." She put a hand on the unfinished white walls. "What do you think of the place?"

"I'm not sure what to think, really. It is filthy." His eyes meandered. "What happened to that large house with the roof?"

"My parents' house, well my mother's. Anyway, it was

too 'high society' for me." She donned a mischievous look. "Also, they kicked me out when I found work as a nurse. They wanted me to marry and look after an estate. I, on the other hand, want to help people. That's what makes me happy."

Death noted how proud she looked. He was confused, to say the least, not having any real notion of the inner workings of human society; especially not the parental aspect. Was it that humans looked after one another until they reached maturity? Or were parents more like patrons, or overseers?

"And being happy involves this space...how? Does the dust give you some form of self-actualization? Do these shredded walls withhold something of sentimental importance or some mystery?"

Robinette shook her head playfully. "Always so dramatic. But no, your poetics are misplaced."

He raised an eyebrow. *Poetics?*

Robinette inched closer to where Death stood in the center of the room. Her stride was casual, and her eyes appraising. "My dear childhood friend owns the building. He's quite an industrious person, you see. That is, he's without a prestigious name, but that doesn't matter anymore. The order of things is changing. Human society is coming to a point where anyone can pursue what means most to them. I want to be a part of a world where everyone chases purpose relentlessly." She stood tall atop the creaky wooden floor and pointed down. "And it all starts with each of us standing on our own two feet!"

Now, Death was utterly lost. *Order has changed? Standing on one's own two feet?* He furrowed his brow, fully displaying how little he understood what Robinette had said.

"Okay, I can tell that was a bit too much. For now, you need to know that this is the point in my life where I take a risk. This place is mine, and it is called possibility."

"Possibility?"

"Possibility," she confirmed. Robinette strode toward him and reached out. A single dainty finger touched Death's forehead. "See it. See the apartment for what it could be."

~~~~

Natural light flowed into the room, and the glistening hardwood floors were reflective. The walls were re-painted white for the most part, with the windowless left side wall accenting the room with a mural. Wafting blues hung below a sea of stars, and the sun's rays lit up a grassy meadow. Mountain flowers—yellow, blue, and pink—were abundant, and trees branched out over shaded areas. Down the hill, there was a stream where all life thrived. Deep greens and blues contrasted the rushing whites that contrasted gray stone.

Along the back wall, the wood stove was well-kept but held no flames at this time. There were newly installed white cabinets nearby with shining brass handles. Nearby, a well-polished wooden table stood waist-high, with four chairs to match.

On the near side of the room, there were a half dozen people about—several little humans running around with bare chubby feet. There were no boxes to trip over, and the floor didn't rattle with every step. The lot of them made the most of the cozy space, and Robinette minded her rocking chair in the corner, with a leather-bound book in her lap.

Death could see the contentment, and the joy. Then, he saw something that surprised him. On the other side of the room was a very human version of himself: bald, dark skin, intense eyes. This version of himself wore suspenders and a white shirt, like so many of the human males that came to his pharmacy in recent times. His human self simply looked across the room and smiled—a smile that was neither crooked nor menacing—aimed kindly at Robinette.

~ ~ ~ ~

He came to, and Robinette stood before him in the same dusty apartment. She gave him a knowing look now.

Why was I there? He looked down at the dainty human woman. *Why was I with her?*

"This place can be a home," Robinette said.

A home... Death thought about what he had seen. It had seemed so warm and inviting. Having a space like that would be a comfort, surely. It wasn't like his pharmacy where Death was always at work. It was a place where he could rest, and leave his obligations at the door. And he could remain with her.

"What about the little humans?" he asked.

"I'm not sure what you mean. Did you imagine little humans?"

Death gulped at that. So, he was the one picturing the possibilities.

Robinette continued. "I didn't expect to go into this so soon, but you probably need to know how humans are made."

"How humans are made?"

"Yes," she said, sighing. "We're going to have to move on. It might be a bit shocking for you, and I've been dreading it."

Move on? He had the sudden urge to shake his head at that. Some yearning welled up inside of him. *We cannot go yet....*

"It can't be helped. So..."

"Wait!" Death's interruption was louder than he meant. "I cannot stand this place. Really, it is so unclean."

Robinette didn't appear to follow. Instead, she seemed put off.

"I mean to say that I want to stay here and tidy up for a bit. I can't leave any place like this. I'm Death. I'm supposed to bring order to things."

Robinette was surprised by that, her face flushed. It was the only surprise that he had managed to pull from her thus far, and seemingly over such a simple thing, too. Maybe not so simple to Death though. He wanted to stay, yes, but he wanted to stay here with her. He wanted to stay here with her for as long as possible, and he had no clue as to why.

"Okay," she managed. "I'm in no hurry after all. I'll just move us on after we're done here."

Death wore his majorly imperfect smile. "Right."

CHAPTER **NINE**

Death opened his eyes to a crowded white room, not so unlike his pharmacy in its ambience, but feeling more like one of his compounding rooms. Light blue cabinets adorned the near side wall with a long counter at waist height, the likes of which had a metallic bowl and faucet built into the smooth composite surface. A freckled woman laid in a bed at the center of the room, with her legs spread under a quilted blue blanket. Messy auburn hair spread out across a cushion, knots indicating a long struggle. Her face was exasperated and red, and her breath labored from physical stress. Sweat poured down her forehead, moving over protruding veins to coalesce at her brow.

Pain, Death thought to himself, surprised by his knowledge of the word. He had only ever seen some semblance of fear in his pharmacy, but he had never been introduced to the concept of pain before. *This is pain. Her physical form is enduring substantial stress.* He watched further. *It harms them. Makes them fear. And then what comes?*

He glanced at the array of humans at the bedside, all of them dutiful and comforting. One stuck out as familiar. The petite blonde woman wore feminine white medical scrubs and a white cap that had a thick red cross at its center. She stood at the head of the bed, where she gave verbal directions to the overexerted woman. Robinette commanded the room. Her face portrayed a new seriousness that Death had yet to observe from her. Whatever was happening was surely of the utmost importance.

Then, there was screaming, and Death suddenly felt like a waste of precious space. People rushed past him often, carrying either receptacles filled with liquid or linen. The woman on the bed looked as though she was holding her breath while she yelled out. She huffed and puffed with such emphasis that Death found himself flushed. Both of her hands desperately gripped the bedside, her forearms bulging, and knuckles turned white. This human said words that Death had no definition for, and gave him pleading looks for which he had no answers.

He looked again to the only human he knew. *Robinette.... What is this? Have you brought me here to show me the human tolerance for pain? Or is this something else entirely?*

Robinette grabbed the woman's hand and beamed the woman a bold look. "All right, Rosemary. We're going to push now."

The woman must have obliged because there was more screaming that followed.

"Again," Robinette demanded.

High-pitched wails of agony made Death's ears ring. His eyes blurred, head spinning. He balled his fists tight, but refused himself the opportunity to look away.

Something is happening. Death's eyes were wide. *Something big.*

And then it came. A small, bald, infantile human, whose skin was more red than any human he had witnessed before. Its tiny eyes were struggling to open, and it squirmed at the gentlest touch. It shrieked as though the shock of its own creation was a terrifying endeavor.

Death's jaw hung below his collar bone. He couldn't fully comprehend what he had just seen. A human was thrust into existence before his very eyes. He looked to Robinette for some assurance. Instead, he found remorse.

Robinette slowly coursed her fingers through the woman's thick auburn hair. On the bed, her patient laid pale—a drastic change from the previously flushed tone— and the blue eyes stared directly at Death. Robinette dropped her head for a moment and said something under her breath.

I know this sensation. Death looked at the sprawled woman's eyes. *I know that expression.* He recalled the fear that creatures had displayed when they looked at him. All of them were unbothered until he snatched them from the line. He struck fear in the hearts of all mortals, save one.

Robinette pushed her head into the shoulder of the woman. The rest of the occupants cleared the room, leaving her alone with the woman and Death.

The Pharmacist walked as softly as he could manage, so to not insult the moment with the clamor of his sleek shoes. He moved closer. Guilt weighed him down with each step. He knew that on the other side of the planar split, he had ripped this woman from the line and turned her into that brilliant blue dust that he had so cherished.

Robinette looked up at him. "Do you remember her?"

The question struck Death at his core. He didn't remember taking this human. He had taken so many.

Death started, "I've been the end of so many...."

"No." Robinette stood, and looked up at him with wet eyes. "Do you remember *her*?" The extra emphasis made Death question his answer. "You ran with us through the meadow. You drenched us in the creek."

The realization washed over Death like the cold stream he had tramped through not so long ago. The auburn hair, rosy cheeks, freckles, and blue eyes. He looked down at the face of that child who had once welcomed him as a friend.

"Do you remember how she waved to you? She wouldn't see you again until just now." Robinette choked her words as she wiped her reddened eyes. "It's just a flash for you, but it is a lifetime for us. Really, how long do you think a year in the living world is to you? A day in your pharmacy? A week?"

The Pharmacist was stunned. "I don't know what to tell you."

"Don't tell me anything then. Just mourn her. Mourn her from now on." She grabbed his hand and squeezed it tighter than she had ever done before. "Mourn all of them if you can. You're connected to every living creature, Death. Every living creature. Why do you think I've taken you this far?"

He paused. "I'm not certain."

"Because you deserve better. You deserve to know the extent of your impact on all life." She nodded to herself as though she was processing what she was saying as it came

74

out. "It's a loss. And it needs to be treated like a loss. There needs to be empathy, yes. But there is more to it than that. The passing of life is also a celebration for what has been left behind for the rest of us. A celebration for each individual, because they have all left ripples that touch those of us that remain. Those ripples even touch you."

"What ripples?" He asked. "I don't understand."

"I know you don't understand." She softened her grip on his hand. "I know. And I'm sorry you don't grasp everything right now."

That type of response was something he might have expected the Doctor to condescend to him with. Robinette's tone was completely different. It was as though she meant to soothe him. It was as though his lack of understanding was an ailment that would be fixed in time. Robinette was never harsh toward him despite, by Death's understanding, having every right to be. He was the scourge of all living creatures. He had just seen his work from the other side. Death was a killer. He was *the* killer.

"You know," Robinette started. "Revisiting this moment didn't make it any easier."

"What do you mean?"

Robinette ignored him. Instead, she looked up, seemingly at the plain white ceiling. "I know it is crucial."

Death stood there, confused, but deciding not to interrupt. He had no intention of trying to dominate this moment. He had no intention of pressing her for an explanation.

Robinette re-oriented herself, wiping pink eyes and standing tall. "It is important that you remember what you saw here. Life was made and taken all at once. It's delicate. It's special."

Death nodded, though he still didn't fully comprehend what she meant. He took another look at the deceased human. This prompted Robinette to lead him to Rosemary's bedside, where he was able to implant a more thorough image of her in his mind. He imagined the mischievous little girl that had goaded him into playfulness. The green dress she wore was more fitting of an image than the loose white gown she adorned.

"I prefer to see the little girl," he exclaimed.

"So do I." Robinette bit her lip. "So would anyone that knew her."

Death shook his head. "I didn't know her."

"She was one of three people who you might have regarded as a friend. I know that. So did she."

He took the moment in. His stomach felt tangled, yet hollow at the same time. Death's chest was heavy and his lips were prominently descending his face.

Robinette patted the tall dark figure on the back. "Come with me, I need you to see one more thing before we go."

She led Death out of the room and into a long sterile-smelling hallway. There were four chairs against the near side wall where a man sat alone. He held his head in his hands, sobbing to himself, seemingly doing his best to not moan in agony. No human in passing dared approach him. The man had the look of someone who had lost the pigment in his skin, but not in the same way as Rosemary. He was crumbling from within.

"Don't look too long at him," Robinette said. "I just wanted to address one final thing before we leave."

Death looked up at her.

"I was young when my father died. I was just sitting

outside a room, much like this. He was calling to me and I couldn't stomach going in to see him at the end. You know what I'm talking about, right?"

Death bit his bottom lip to keep it from quivering. He knew exactly what she was talking about. He could still see the man in the tag, calling out from a dirty bed. The Doctor had explained it to him even, and he had dismissed it in the moment.

"My father dying, that was inevitable. He was sick and old, and had a lot of good in his life before the end."

Death dropped his head.

"Look at me." Robinette kept her eyes wide, serious, and explicit.

Death did as he was told, though the weight of his head was unbearable at this time.

"I forgive you for taking my father's life."

"What?"

"My father. I forgive you. And I will forgive you for Rosemary before this is over. Dying is inevitable, but life isn't taken freely. There is an etiquette to what you do. You understand, right?"

It was at this time that Death let his head fall onto Robinette's shoulder. She embraced him, through all the shock and dread that coursed through the dark entity's body and soul. She embraced him.

"Don't hate me, Death. Don't take my words as being harsh. I had no choice but to show you this. That's why I wanted to show you all of the good before now. There's just no build-up to these types of things. I learned that when my father died. I learned that when I became a nurse, when I decided my purpose was to help and nurture people."

Again, Death didn't know how to respond. He felt utterly dismayed.

"I feel as sorry as you do." She took a deep breath. "Don't falter, okay?"

"I wish I hadn't known until now," Death replied half-heartedly. "But something was there, and I just didn't want to see it."

Robinette stepped back from the embrace, grabbing and squeezing Death's large hands. "There is more to see, Death. More good. So, come on. We still have a few more stops to make."

Death clenched his jaw. He wanted to separate himself from the situation, but he was too deep now. He turned to face his small guide. Eagerly, he squeezed her hands before putting them over his eyes.

CHAPTER **TEN**

This time, Death was no longer enclosed. He was once again in nature, with stunted blades of grass just grazing the tops of his soles. The ground was flat, and the flora was all clean-shaven and symmetrical. Red, pink, and white flowers were bundled together and set out on display at various points meant to catch the eye. Humans had clearly managed the life in this area for beautification purposes. Death couldn't decide whether the unnatural alteration was a good thing or not. To him, one species dominating another was interesting. The concept itself had potential—potential for order, but also for chaos.

White chairs were arranged in asymmetrical rows, all of which were claimed by humans that adorned formal clothes. They faced a grand gazebo, also white, and its pillars were intertwined with green vines that bloomed dark red rose buds. The gazebo overlooked an expansive and flowing surface that reflected golden light. That surface reminded Death of the stream, clearly liquid, though it was wide and its borders reached the far side horizon.

At the head of the gazebo was a wizen-faced man dressed in all black save for a slim white collar folded at the base of his neck. His dark hair was receding, and he kept his face clean. His eyes were peeled as though he was constantly suspicious of his surroundings. He looked out among a forming crowd expectantly.

Death recognised the other man under the gazebo. It was the same man from the hospital, but more lively. It hadn't been until now that Death had really looked at him. The man was not yet middling in age, wearing a fitted black suit and tie. His face was sharp, and the shadow of his brow deep. That large nose and those muddled green eyes hadn't changed, he was the mischievous boy that Death had met on that grassy slope.

Death's heart skipped a beat.

The boy from the grassy slope had become the man who had collapsed from grief, one wall separating him from Rosemary's deathbed. But now... He was more himself again.

A girl, who couldn't have been a handful of years old, walked down an aisle of sleek white fabric. Her flowing brown hair was tied up, but Death could recognise that the curls had fought all attempts to tame them. The dress she wore was white, and a lacy skirt flowered out to her ankles. She looked back for a moment, observing the large gathering of humans with apprehension. Her deep blue eyes looked back at Death, who took note of her rosy complexion and freckles. She pinched her eyes together and smiled with baby teeth before turning back. She meandered down the aisle until she came to the man who Death knew from the start of his journey. Robinette's dear friend had grown up, and the young girl was his. Her chubby little hands reached for the man's, and he embraced her at his side.

I think I understand. Death had failed to recognise Rosemary when she had died in that room, but he wouldn't fail to remember her kin. He looked the man in the suit up and down. *So they were companions of sorts, and he inherited the young one.*

Thrums echoed through the air, and the masses stood. They looked back, seemingly at Death, who felt small under the weight of such an extensive audience. And how should he react? These humans were too numerous for him to interact with. It was not as though he could split himself to match their number, not on this side of the planar split. And even if he could, what would he do? Death was not mortal. He was not human. So, he grabbed the only instinct that presented itself. Death dropped his head as though he meant to hide in plain sight, all the while doubting that such camouflage was possible. He just hoped that they were looking past him.

From his peripherals, the Pharmacist noticed he wasn't alone. Turning, he found Robinette, who glided through space until she stood shoulder to shoulder with him. Death's heart sprung from his chest when he saw her. Gossamer material sprouted from her vibrant upturned hair and hung to veil her face. White silk was fitted to her torso, with short sleeves capping her shoulders. The rest of her gown flowed down the rest of her like waves. She stood almost to his chin now, so she must have had heels, though her feet were obscured within the depths of her skirt.

She turned to him and held out her arm. "Would you mind walking me? We can share a few words on our way, but there isn't much time."

Death's jaw dropped. His dark eyes moved slowly, but not slower than his mind. It was as though he was moving through time and space at a drastically reduced rate. Something about this moment felt remorseful, but only to him. All the humans were cheerful. It was another thing about them that he couldn't relate to.

He reluctantly linked arms with her, and they began down the aisle. Each step was heavy, and the people around them were drowned out by his blurred vision and the steady ambience.

Death took this time to speak: "Robinette," he whispered. "What is this?"

She didn't look at him, but answered him nonetheless, "This is a wedding. It joins two humans as partners and lovers. This one is mine."

Death nodded in the man's general direction. "And him?"

"Jeffrey. You know him from the creek." She paused. "And the hospital." She took a moment to recover before continuing, "And the little delight at his hip is his daughter, Mary Jane. You were there when she was born. I know we were just there, but really, it has been some time since then."

"Of course." Death graced the aisle with shame. He had killed the girl's mother during the moment of her creation. That surely left a mark on the young human, for it had certainly left an impression on Death. Was that why Robinette was binding herself to Jeffrey and his child? Was it because Death had taken Rosemary? Robinette had to fill in somewhere, to keep balance. Death understood balance, at least, he thought he did.

"Do you remember when I spoke to you about purpose?"

"Yes," Death answered.

"That little girl is everything to me. My purpose, as I have found, was to nurse the sick and mend the helpless. And there is no greater sickness than growing up without a parent. Do you understand?"

No. Of course not. Despite his confusion, Death nodded.

"Rosemary was my best friend. Jeffrey is a fine man, friend, and partner. But Mary Jane, she is the future. I have to be there to guide her."

Thanks to what I've done...

He looked around at all the humans who watched him and Robinette traverse the foreground of this occasion. They varied in age, texture, enthusiasm, size. He would take them all one day, disintegrating them into a blue compound that would be recycled to those that came after. They were not his kind, and so they could never truly know the extent of his burden. In truth, Death himself was still learning the innate sadness of his personage. Now, as he walked the only human he had known intimately to her joining ceremony, he felt the sting of such sadness. Even worse, he had no clue as to why he felt this way.

Robinette came up beside Jeffrey, under the tall arching dome of the white gazebo. She motioned for Death to move to the far left, to which he obliged. He stood beside the climbing pink roses. They faced away from him, their refined scent wafting toward and encircling Robinette and Jeffrey. Even flora seemed to understand that his presence was indicative of a thorough breakdown of one's existential integrity.

Death glanced down at his life essence drenched hands. *I understand. I'm a killer.* The Pharmacist sighed, and he forced the return of his gaze.

Robinette smiled at her tall, well-dressed counterpart. Little Mary Jane stirred, and before anyone could mutter a word, she grabbed Robinette's hand and enveloped it with her father's. The crowd swooned when they saw this, and even Death couldn't help but sense the preciousness of her action.

The man in all black moved forward with a leather-bound book in hand. He was stern, seemingly unfazed by the moment. His wrinkled forehead and darkly shaded brow resonated an unwelcome aura. The man's place above all the other humans made him seem untouchable, not so unlike Death.

His voice was coarse, but firm. "Dearly beloved, we have gathered you here today to join these two people in matrimony, for all time in the presence of God. The decision to marry is not one made lightly, and it is an eternal bond that transcends even death."

Death raised his brow at that last line. This man was wrong. These deep-seated human superstitions and rituals were so very wrong when it came to the end of one's existence. Nothing transcended him. He knew the end. He was that end. Death gritted his teeth, and endured this alleged authority's supposition for the sake of Robinette and Mary Jane.

"If anyone has reason to object to the union of these two people, speak now or forever hold your peace."

Death felt the urge well up inside his stomach. He

wanted more than anything to take Robinette away from the others. He wanted to bring her back to times before and stay there. He wanted to dance, run through grass mounds, have in-depth conversations about existentialism and destiny. He wanted to feel her gentle touch against his eyelids as she took him along the timeline of her life.

Still, he held his tongue. Death knew that she deserved better than an eternity with him, merely floating around his pharmacy like a mismatched ornament. He now knew that he wasn't as perfect as he had once claimed to be. The "order" he craved was an illusion. Death was just an obsessive gatekeeper at the edge of reality, who reveled in filling his jars with the life essence he stole from mortals.

Robinette's emerald eyes had seen through him, and she had chosen her path. Death glanced at the bright little girl at Robinette's side. She had chosen right.

Death closed his eyes. The dark underside of his eyelids beat back the image of the mortal union, and he forced the gruff voice of the official from his mind. Soon, he heard nothing except tapping, and felt nothing but cold.

CHAPTER **ELEVEN**

Liquid fell from the bleak ceiling overhead, and plump condensed fog rumbled and swayed while shutting out the radiant golden light that Death had come to know. Small eruptions burst from the amorphous fog cover, and the Pharmacist was constantly forced to blink his eyes dry. His nose ran and the smell of cold air frazzled him. In a matter of moments, his umbral lab coat had become soaked, and his white scrubs were tarnished where they weren't translucent. Air lifted the black flaps that hung past his waist, and stung the skin that stuck to his wet clothes. His heels dug into extra soft ground, this plane being more muck than grass. No life grew here save for the grass and some measure of wilting flora along a black spiraled fence, being too decrepit to identify. Surely, he had already taken those plants on his side of the planar split.

All around him were sleek stone pillars and slabs, the likes of which had human symbols carved into their surfaces—some form of identification to distinguish them from each other. The sizes varied from being lower than Death's knees to just above his sternum, and they were all the same wet gray—a familiar tone that reminded the Pharmacist of his line. The shadows cast by these stone slabs blended with the dismal ambience caused by the dark overcast.

This place felt familiar to Death, like he fit inside its borders. Considering that he was the end of all things, the scenery seemed apt for him to make an appearance. The surrounding area matched his eeriness and his newfound brooding. That brooding came from the growing realization of who he was, and what he meant to mortals. It came from his inability to be human—his inability to be with her.

Robinette. Death pictured her reflective green eyes. They were perfectly cut gems, with no muddled features nor blemishes. They saw through him every time she turned his way. *You've taken me this far. I'm not sure if I should resent you for what has happened. You added some vulnerability that I can't pinpoint. It's something that not even I can kill.*

He looked around for her. So far he hadn't seen anyone, and this environment didn't seem to suit Robinette. She was too optimistic, too passionate, and yet she had brought him here, right?

No....

She hadn't been the one to close his eyes during the wedding. Perhaps that didn't matter, but he couldn't know for sure. Death squinted and dropped his head to avoid any liquid falling from the sky that might obscure his vision. He scanned the area again.

Where is she? He wondered. *Her bright yellow hair*

should stand out among all this drab. Death made another passing glance.

In the distance, a crowd of humans appeared, walking through the heavy air with their heads down. All of them seemed to wear black clothing, without any of the dozens of people from their ranks breaking from that norm. The women wore dark netted shawls that covered their faces and the caps they had donned for the occasion. Most men were in suits, not so different from the ones worn at the wedding Death had just witnessed, but without flowers, and without color variance in their belts and ties. Four men, in particular, led the pack as they carried a long wooden box by the silver grips attached to its side. The men were unextraordinary in their appearance, all middling height and age, but the box they carried was like a beacon in this cold eerie place. The box must have been as long as Death was tall, and it was lacquered to the point of shining despite the lack of overhead light. And people followed it—all of them trudging after it without fail, as though they were its backline escorts. Upon witnessing this, Death decided that whatever was being carried was of the utmost importance.

As more people emerged from the rainy haze, Death took note of three particular individuals. He knew them. One was the girl, Mary Jane, who had grown considerably. Her baby features had gone: her cheekbones higher on her face, fingers thinned out, and hair down to her thighs. She was easily as tall as Robinette was, but not fully mature yet.

How long has it been? Death had just seen her as a child, and now she was at the end of her adolescence. *How far forward?*

Mary Jane was alongside her kin and creator, Jeffrey, and she kept her head tight against his torso while he held up some rod that had a circular cover at its head, thus preventing the two of them from getting wet. Jeffrey's eyes were red, in the very same way Robinette's were when Rosemary was killed. Just behind them was the official in all black save for his collar. He walked without a cover and was seemingly unnerved by the climate that drenched him.

So, this is more sadness. More loss. Death eyed the wizen-faced official. *Perhaps another unnerving address.* He reviewed the remaining humans in the hope of spotting Robinette. *Why are you separate from your kin?*

Death migrated in the general direction of the humans, staying just on the outskirts of their collective. Hopefully, this way he would eventually run into Robinette. She usually found him anyway.

None in the group spoke, but some of them muffled their weeping. Death did his best to ignore being affected by these heavy human emotions. After all, he had already let himself feel too much.

Continuing on, the group ended up at a site that boasted symmetrically dug ground and surrounding chairs. Its depth was unmeasurable to Death from where he stood, but he imagined that he could fit his entire body in it several times over, prone or otherwise. At its head, there was another slab that was more like white marble than gray stone. It had more human symbols to mark the plot, and Death found himself wishing that he could interpret these symbols because he desperately needed clarification.

The box was lowered into the hole, with great care by

several individuals. Once in, the box could only be seen by looking over the threshold of cut ground. Next, the humans took their seats, and the official stood at the head of the ditch. The man raised his black leather book from his chest and dropped his head.

He cleared his throat, and started with that gruff tone of his, "Robinette Marie Wright, formerly known as Robinette Marie Black, was a fine woman, and so much more to the people who knew her."

Death's ears perked up at that. *Was?*

"She was a mother to a beautiful daughter." The official nodded at Mary Jane before looking at Jeffrey. "A devoted wife." He paused again. "Robinette was a loving person who put others before herself. As a nurse, family member, friend, and upstanding member of the community. Her life has touched many others, and her memory will continue to do so."

The man looked down at the box now. Death's eyes widened as he realized the purpose of this human ritual.

"Here she lays, forever in the eyes of God, until she is reborn. May she rest in peace."

The official muttered some words from his book that the other humans repeated. Death had no interest in what the man's book said, for he knew what was on the other side of the planar split.

I didn't touch her yet...I hadn't even taken her to the compounding room. Death's jaw shuddered. *What is this?*

After the official retreated from the foreground, Mary Jane stood and walked to the head of the ditch. She held a yellow mountain flower—the same type of yellow as Robinette's hair. Quietly, the girl said some words to herself and dropped the flower into the ditch, where it landed atop the long wooden box. Afterward, she looked at Death, and gave a consoling smile, much like the ones he had received from Robinette. The smile neither implied nor elicited happiness for either of them, but was necessary as Mary Jane understood Death in a way that the other humans did not. She got that from Robinette.

The fact that Mary Jane reminded Death of her was just a small comfort, which didn't compare to the ripping that Death felt in his chest. The sensation was his first experience with real emotional pain, and it was not an easy introduction. His muscles ached and shivered, and his head felt swollen, especially behind his eyes.

Jeffrey approached the head of the ditch and embraced his daughter, who was unmoving. He dropped flowers, all the while sniffling. Then he nodded at Death, but gave no smile. He put his hand at the arch of his daughter's back, and ushered her from where she stood. The pair of them walked back to their seats, and others took their place.

It was only at this moment that Death realized just how many people had come to this ritual on Robinette's behalf. There were more than a few dozen, if not over a hundred humans gathered to bury one of their own. Death knew that was an important detail that he was meant to take note of, but he couldn't flesh out his thoughts.

There is no other line of reasoning that fits. I must have killed her....

The Pharmacist pictured his naked hands touching Robinette's warm skin. He imagined the feeling of the blue compound she would become, and how it would slip through his fingers and fall into a jar that was composed of all the sentient creatures he had taken. He saw her being lost in that jar, forever.

His thoughts lingered.

Death still stood when the sky began to clear and the humans vacated the hallowed ground. It was at this time that he approached the recently filled ditch cautiously. He looked down at the fresh mound, now knowing why the box was as long as he was tall. He grabbed a leftover mountain flower and twirled it in his hands. It was blue like the life essence that was so crucial to the existence of all creatures. He placed it gingerly on top of the thick burial mound.

Despite there being no liquid falling from above, Death felt a wet substance course down his left cheek and split at the edge of his lips. He endured the salty taste at the rim of his mouth. More droplets descended from the depths of his eyes, and he shut his eyes to make them stop.

CHAPTER **TWELVE**

Death didn't need to readjust his eyes upon opening them, as his soft gray surroundings were an amicable transition from the cover of his eyelids. Two of his duplicates were at his sides, and they all looked on at the examination table at the center of the room where Robinette laid prone, her eyes reflecting off the speckless glass jar that was filled with life essence base. The sight of her lightweight body sprawled across seamless black leather was a bludgeon that shattered the haze that had overtaken Death. It was at this point that the reality of recent moments hit him— all of it by his own hands and through his own eyes.

While his mind was away, Death had walked Robinette to the back of his pharmacy, past the white door and through the consuming darkness that made the path to the compounding room that they now occupied. His duplicates had done what they did best and prepared Robinette for the administration of a lethal touch by strapping her down. The ebony skin of the original's naked right hand was free from the restraints of stained gloves, and his eyes were jet blue with his sclera fully consumed.

His duplicates looked at him, the original Death, and they had now gained the knowledge of his time on the other side of the planar split. Every Death shared wide eyes, and beamed them back at Robinette, who was in a lull.

Seeing what had happened, Death wanted to lash out. He wanted to enact some manner of wrath built up inside him, but at who? Who allowed this save for himself? It was he who had strapped that gentle Robinette down upon her would-be deathbed.

The original turned to his other selves and echoed a thought across their shared consciousness: *Leave! Attend to others!*

His duplicates made themselves scarce and wandered back into the abyss between the compounding rooms and the pharmacy counter. Then, Death released his power on Robinette, thus allowing her to slowly regain her faculties. He unstrapped her too, not wanting to keep her bound in any way. His eyes returned to their normal state by the time Robinette came around. She sat up and gave Death an inquisitive look.

"Where are we?"

Death sighed. He showed her his back and walked to the corner of the room. He braced his head with his gloved left hand and muttered to himself, "I was going to kill her..."

"Death." She called after him. After he failed to respond, her bantam feet sounded against the sleek gray floor of the compounding room. "Come on. Don't tell me that a being as powerful as Death is having a nervous breakdown."

This isn't the way things were meant to be. He pictured himself lulling her into another trance and walking her back to the line. It might take a while for him to find her prescription, but his reach was infinite here. In the worst-case scenario, he could give her some of the life essence he had hoarded as a result of the recent quell. Or he could keep Robinette here with him, and bear the guilt and shame of ripping her from the life she had built.

Death dropped his hands into the folds of his lab coat. He tapped his sleek shoes while the possibilities swarmed him. Emotions were cluttered, too complex for his rudimentary understanding of them to be of any great help. He was lost.

There was a delicate touch on his shoulder followed by an even softer voice: "Hey. You're too uneasy. Talk with me."

Death turned slowly. His brow dropped forcibly on the circles of his eyes, and his teeth vised together. He displayed his ungloved hand just inches from his torso.

"Do you know what happens here?" He let the weight of his brow diminish just slightly. "I've told you what my touch brings, Robinette. You can see what you would have become in that damned jar!"

"Death," She shook her head.

"I saw them perform a ritual. On the other side. I saw them put a box into the ground and say goodbye. We need to stop that from happening!"

"My life has ended on the other side already. Don't you see? I said it from the beginning. I was sent here to die. On the way over here, you checked my prescription. Come on, think back to that moment."

"What are you talking about?" He recoiled.

"Don't mute it out. Just revisit the recent memory."

She put a single finger on his forehead, much like she had done when she showed him her apartment. Death didn't transfer his consciousness across the planar split, nor did he see any future possibilities. Rather, his mind's eye was sent back in time, when he had moved Robinette beyond his ebony counter.

~~~~

Death came into his original body, though it was minutes prior. He stood alongside the gray-washed creatures that formed an aisle against the great marble surface that held subsequent fills of life essence. At his other side was the small blonde woman he had come to know, and three copies of himself who wore smug expressions—all of whom, through their shared consciousness, entertained curiosity regarding how it might feel to quell a self-aware being.

Robinette was cognisant at this time, and had willingly obeyed Death's commands to follow him to the very front top of the sleek black threshold. He had moved a striped arachnid, the likes of which fit in the center of his palm, and guided Robinette to take the creature's place in line. His intention was to determine how the pharmacy would react to a being who disrupted the flow of the line. Clearly, her place was lost among the masses, so this experiment had become inevitable.

When he placed her, her eyes had lit up—the bright emeralds beneath her brow reflecting the luminescent blue orb before her. Then, something unexpected took place. The receptacle had changed tags and emptied itself of the life essence it previously held. The receptacle now belonged to Robinette, and it showed no refill.

Surprise washed over Death and his duplicates, and they had all shared a knowing look. This was evidence of a system that remained undiscovered until the unprecedented encounter with a conscious being—a system in which the pharmacy automatically corrected the order of its line.

This meant that Robinette had to die.

~~~~

Death opened his eyes and peered down at Robinette, her knowing expression drawing desperation from him. He was in awe at first, but his mind began to ping with questions and opposing solutions: *Would it matter if I found her original place in line? Would I be able to offer her pure compound? I could dose it manually....enough to keep her living anyway. But then I'd lose her. But she'd still be her.*

"Your mind is still running wild." Her hands reached for his, but he rejected what would be a lethal touch. She kept her voice steady. "Slow it down."

"Robinette, I don't want to kill you. Really, it is the furthest thing from what I want." He let out an exasperated breath. "If I have to choose, then I choose to not ever touch you with these hands."

"I don't know if you can make that choice."

"I can if I am as powerful as I should be!" Death clenched his jaw, curling his brow and balling his fists so tight that his arms shook. He felt a new mix of several emotions well up inside him: anger, fear, and helplessness. He found that each corroded the core of his being, and this feeling was elevated when the emotions were in tandem with one another. Anger drew from fear. Fear drew from helplessness. Death felt like he was shattering slowly from within.

"And what about the order of things? You told me that you bring order. From your position as the Pharmacist who maintains a balance between existence and non-existence, how can you justify keeping me alive when you have snuffed the lives of others? How can you pick and choose?"

"I didn't choose this, though! I was told to take a tenth of the human population regardless of their prescription." His eyes felt heavy. He thought back to the overwhelming pleasure he felt every time that blue powder fell through his fingers and into one of his glass jars. He thought about why he, as the original, refrained from doing the deed. It was too intoxicating. "I picked them at random. I've never once killed a creature because I wanted to see it suffer."

"You mentioned a thrill once."

Death's eyes widened. His lips curled as his own words came back on him, and he replied in the only way he could. "Not from making the living suffer me. The fulfillment has always been elsewhere." He leered at the jar.

"And what if I suffer for living past my time? Would you choose that for me? Would that fulfill you?"

Death remained silent.

"Death, you know what has to be done. My prescription cannot be refilled!"

"It can!" Death burst from his passive stance in the

corner of the room and moved past Robinette until he stood before the jar of cobalt compound material. He looked down at it, its vibrant blue glow mesmerizing him the longer he stared. "I can give you what I took."

"What?" Her voice got higher.

Death turned. "Really. I can give you some of the excess from the quell of humans. It will work."

Robinette peeled back, and her face boasted some emotion between skepticism and disgust. She shook her head.

"Robinette..."

"No!"

Death dropped his head, and walked to the center of the room where he sat on his own examination bed. He slumped his long torso, and the bottom of his legs molded the soft black leather. His feet just barely glanced the ground, his ankles hovering. He felt lost.

Robinette approached, still without unease. She stood before him and placed her left hand on his knee. She leaned forward just slightly.

"Do you remember what I said to you when we danced? That we humans base our lives on finding what our purpose is. That our purpose isn't defined for us like yours is." Her grip on Death's knee firmed. "Remember, it takes a lifetime for a human to discover what they are meant for. A lifetime to come to some conclusion as to why they exist. If I take that excess life meant for something or someone else, what chance do I give them of having a full life? Where are the possibilities for them in that scenario? Human or other. How much disorder am I worth? How much corruption to the balance between the living and the dead?"

Robinette shook her head and continued, "I'm not. I'm just one of many, and I owe my life to the whole."

"And what of your sense of purpose? Don't you see!? I'm offering you the chance to seek it! To be with Mary Jane and Jeffrey! To meet me later on!"

"Death, my life has come to its final chapter, like my father and Rosemary. No one can hang on to me, just like I couldn't hang on to them." She aimed a glance over at the jar. "My life now belongs to something bigger than myself, and there is no greater purpose than that."

"I see." His voice broke apart as he spoke. He really was incapable of convincing her, wasn't he? No appeal to her sense of self-preservation would work, not on Robinette. She was special in that way. "If that's what you want, and it must be done to maintain order, then I..."

Death shut his mouth. Instead, he stood and motioned for her to lay on the leather examination bed—the simple wave of his arm feeling treacherous beneath his skin. His lower jaw remained tight to the ceiling of his mouth, for he had said everything he knew to say.

Before laying down, Robinette embraced Death, her thin arms arcing around his waist and pulling her small form tightly against his. He remained still through the embrace, worried that any movement he made would cue her to release him. And so, they remained close for a few prolonged moments.

"Do you remember when I told you that I'd forgive you for Rosemary before this was all over?" Robinette looked up at him, seeing through his stonewalled expression. "Well, I do."

Death let a tear slip down his cheek.

Robinette continued, "I can see that you are a part of

something bigger than just yourself. It might take a while to see it, but the time will come."

She moved to the examination table and sat upright. She pulled back her yellow hair and laid her head down while spreading her short legs across the table. Then Robinette reached out for Death's sleeve, pulling his ungloved hand toward her eyes.

When he touched her, she smiled up at him. Death looked away, instead focusing on the warmth of her skin as she faded. In mere moments, Death found himself alone again, his free hand filled with the rich cobalt powder that was once his only friend and companion.

He finally let out the gasp that had been growing within his lungs. He shook his head and did his best to hold back the wet eyes he had discovered on the other side of the planar split. And as he dropped Robinette's remains into the jar of blue compound, a few of his tears fell with her.

There, he thought. *You're part of everyone now.*

Death wiped his eyes and hardened the muscles in his face. He took a stern step toward the exit, splitting a new copy of himself from the base of his body before the clack of his heel reverberated back up to his ear. Several more steps, and the original was at the door. He stopped for a moment.

Without turning back, he addressed his other self: "I need you to take over for a while." Then, he continued on.

CHAPTER **THIRTEEN**

Death made his way up the long spiral stairs that led to the Doctor's library. He pushed through the golden fog, stepping swiftly as he fled the memory of Robinette fading away at his touch. He had no tether to his pharmacy anymore, no desire to stay there and continue what seemed so futile. There were other Deaths to take his place, all of them born from his very own consciousness. They even shared his grief, and perhaps they would be better for it, better than he had been as the original; and if they weren't, they could rely on a degree of separation that he didn't have. As the original, he was solely responsible for killing her.

Death emerged upon the marble floor, striding into the stacks. His jaw had remained tense though the entire climb so his nose was heavy with breath. He slowed as he reached the depths of the library, steadying himself for what would surely be a difficult encounter.

Life, the Doctor. You knew this would happen. You know everything. Death peeled his eyes as he rounded a corner. He saw her, sitting on her crystal throne while her riffraff lounged with open books sprawled across the floor. Rather than judging them for their messiness, Death was deeply offended by how they were all so carefree. He beamed an accusatory stare at the Doctor, filling himself with disdain for how her knowledge never seemed to weigh her down.

"Oh, dear," the tall woman said. "I would say this is unexpected, but we all know better. Still, we haven't set a meeting. And it is well known that you resent my company, Death."

"Your omniscience is truly a curse for the likes of me." He meandered the edge of the open foyer, circling as though he was marking out his space. "You have done a lot of wrong."

The Doctor crossed her legs, resetting that long golden lab coat over her knees. "And what makes you think that you know what wrong I have done?" She tilted her head just slightly to reveal a knot of black braided hair. A half-smile crept up the corner of her left cheek. "As I know it, you've done just as much as I have."

"Not knowingly!" He wanted to burst forth at her.

"No, not knowingly. But have you considered that in knowing, you would have made a worse decision?"

"What do you mean?"

"You know now, but look at where you are. Look at the state you are in. You can't operate like this."

He spoke with newfound harshness, "And how is knowing now better than knowing prior? Please, enlighten me, you shameless creature."

The Doctor didn't move, while all but two of her subordinates retreated into the stacks. The two that stayed by her side seemed nothing more than feeble pets, loyal and dominable all the same. The Doctor glowered at Death, eyes seemingly pinpointing his every weakness.

Finally, she spoke, "I'm too intelligent to enforce shame upon myself. It just serves as a hindrance. Also, I'm not going to enlighten you with anything."

He froze.

"You did your job and you killed the girl. It was her time."

"She has a name!" Death shouted.

The Doctor pointed up at the ceiling above, the golden clouds swirling until they formed into Robinette's soft face. "She had a name. Now, she is no longer with the living. I saw clearly what you did to her. The same as anyone who has the misfortune of meeting Death."

Those words cut into Death like hot shrapnel, stopping him utterly. His lower lip curled, jaw shivering and eyes wide.

"What happened to that smug expression you used to wear when you would claim how efficient you were at your job? When you would endlessly gloat about bringing order? What happened to that, Death?"

He whispered with rage, holding himself back fully: "You know what happened..." Death took a few steps closer to his counterpart, passing the cushioned reading areas of her followers. "You're just as responsible as me for everything that has transpired. More so even."

"You speak as though we've come full circle, when in fact we have really just left the middle of this particular chain of events. Should I tell you what is next? Or perhaps you want to wander in your sorrow? Those newfound human emotions would serve you well in that regard."

The matter-of-factness of the Doctor's tone drew out the bottled rage of Death. He strutted from his place at the center of the foyer aggressively while the Doctor sat up expectantly. He burst toward her, his explosive rush only being intercepted by the likes of the Doctor's subordinates. He grabbed one by the throat, while pushing the other aside. He leaned his weight into the nameless ilk of the Doctor, throwing the male to the ground—silver robe fluttering before the boom of his head.

Death stood back up, and took off his left glove, revealing his bare hand. He looked up at the Doctor, into her ever-knowing blue eyes. There was a pause. Death could do it. He was the killer of all beings.

He pointed at her.

"You will mind the way you speak to me from this point forward because I have no qualms with using my bare hands on you. You want to turn to dust. Keep dismissing me!"

The Doctor didn't retreat from the threat, rather she stood tall and glided towards him. It only took a single heartbeat before she was upon him.

Death took a defensive posture as the imposing woman towered against him. He had a split second to make a decision. Looking up at how Robinette's face dissipated from the celestial fog ceiling, he thrust out his hand.

There was a slapping sound, the Doctor recoiling just slightly. Then, she chuckled.

"It's as though I knew that would happen," the Doctor mocked.

"What!?" Death looked down at his gloveless hand.

"Where is your power outside your domain, Death? Touch me all you want. Really. I am more than your equal here."

He took a few steps back, shaking his head. It was at this point that Death noticed all of the woman's contemporaries watching nervously from behind bookshelves. Apparently, his threat had worked on them, up to the point where he had failed to kill the Doctor with his touch. They began to come out, looming like a mob around Death and their mistress.

"All of those human emotions have infected you. You've forgotten so much."

"Stop." He waved his hand forcibly at her again.

The Doctor sighed. "Say you were able to kill me, here and now. You can't, but say you could. In that instance, you would be taking everyone along with me. Billions of the humans you've come to emulate." She wiped the red spot on her cheek where Death had connected. "And that is just the present batch. All of the creatures that would ever have been will cease. Every possible Robinette."

His stomach was turned by her words.

The Doctor continued, "Without an omniscient piece, the balance between existence and non-existence will see a catastrophe. Without me, all living beings will be squandered within a generation. You'd do best to remember who I am when you consider your threats."

He reeled back. "What do you mean by 'every possible Robinette?'"

"I mean that there is a more powerful force at work here, and Robinette won't be the last living being to know Death intimately."

Shock coursed from his neck to his feet. "So, I will meet more?"

"No, I never said that. I said that more living beings would know Death intimately. And the persona of Death transcends you. Have you ever wondered why you are omnipresent? Have you ever thought about what might happen if you, the original, touches himself and dies?"

"It has always been clear that I am omnipresent so that I may handle my workload. What are you trying to imply?"

The Doctor's bright red lips, now slightly smeared, drew up to her high cheekbones. "No implications, dear. Just facts. And the fact is that you are omnipresent so that the consciousness and persona of Death can be reset."

"Reset?"

An elegant stroke of her hand emphasized her next words: "A new original. A new consciousness. You see now, don't you? It's the perfect way to compensate for what would be a poor retention rate of an eternal killer. As a person, you aren't meant to last forever, but the system...now that is a different thing altogether."

He was stricken, physically and mentally. Death reverted to skepticism as a defense. *What if she is lying to me?*

The Doctor drew closer to him, taking the bulk of her space back. She glided in circles around him, narrowing in as though he was prey of sorts. "You may wonder why I have picked this moment for a revelation, or why I have even revealed anything to you. It's natural for you to doubt me at first. And now I ask you to consider that our sole similarity is that we both care about the system. Like you, it is part of my makeup to look after the delicate equilibrium of existence and non-existence."

"Then why would this happen? Why would Robinette show up at all? I was perfectly efficient. You know I was."

"You weren't. You craved imbalance. You craved sole control of the distribution of life essence."

Death lowered his head and stared down at his bright blue gloves, the likes of which were stained with the base compound for life essence. He had yearned for that power, yes. He had welcomed the thrill of deciding whether or not a creature should live. And now he saw how poorly equipped he was for such decisions.

He met the Doctor's cold eyes. "So Robinette was an incentive for me. An incentive for change?"

"The emergence of Robinette was going to yield one of two possibilities. Either you would let go of your controlling nature when you learned the value of life, or you would crumble as you became more human. It is clear by looking at you that the latter has taken place."

"So I'm..."

"Obsolete," she finished. "You are a jam in the machine. For all the humanization you've gained, you are infected with new flaws. Sorrow, greed, anger, and lust, just to name a few." She stopped in front of him, her flowing golden lab coat glistening against the floor's luster. Moving closer, Death could smell her strong flowery scent. "You came here undecided on whether you were going to seek asylum or demand I take responsibility for Robinette's death. But I offer you neither a safe space nor the abolishment of your guilt. Instead, I will give you this advice: go back to your pharmacy and put the system right. Reset Death by taking yourself out of the picture."

"You want me to die?"

The Doctor turned from him quickly and walked back

to her crystal throne. Her lackeys began to emerge from the shadows behind the library's shelves. She was sitting when she addressed him next: "I've said everything I mean to say. It is your time to leave now."

"Fine. I'll sort things out on my own." Death promptly exited the central foyer of the gilded library. His temperament was uneasy, shaking his head, and huffing with anger and disbelief. The self-exiled Pharmacist would have to make his return. He would have to go back to the site where he had murdered so many.

CHAPTER **FOURTEEN**

Emerging from the half black and half white door, Death was greeted by himself. Their two withdrawn looks mirrored each other from forehead to chin, and the hollow feeling inside Death's stomach was equally shared. Exhaustion, not the physical kind, was rampant, and the once self-assured entity was left to wonder why he felt defeat across every joint and limb. The mental wear was powerful, and it left both the original and the copy too little energy to speak out loud like they so often did. Instead, both Deaths communicated through thoughts.

The Doctor. The copy was audible in the mind of the original. *She uses her omniscience to guide us, and we fulfill her most promising outcome whether we like it or not. We can't trust her, but she knows that. And she has planned for an apt reaction on our part. No matter how we move next....*

Both Deaths shook their heads in frustration.

If only I could lure her to my pharmacy, the original thought to himself. *Then maybe she would feel threatened enough to alter her course of action. Her words might be different in such a scenario, but it is too late now. She knows all, and I've been had.*

Both dark enigmatic figures seemed to clench their jaws at the same time. Then, the original willed the words: "I have to reset Death. The pharmacy with me... everything..."

His other self nodded appraisingly at the words as soon as they were said. "You need to die."

Death felt his innards lurch back toward his spine. Now that he faced no other options, mortal terror had risen within him. Dying it turns out, invoked fear from even Death. The idea of non-existence wasn't particularly frightening so much as the prospect of his entire consciousness being lost forever. The role and being of Death would live on in his duplicates, but the persona of the current original would be erased. All of his experience, in the pharmacy and in the human world, would just vanish. His influence on all those he had met—the very ripples of his existence—would surely go with it. What could be more terrifying than that?

He bit his lip in an attempt to repel his unease.

"You know, I am the oldest copy. So..."

"Yes," the original cut in. "You will become the new original. I assume all of the killings done during my time would be remembered as unremarkable and consistent with regard to standard operations. It will be like a distant memory. You'll return to the state you were in before the quell of humanity, and so would all the others."

"Perhaps there would be a slight variation. Otherwise,

what would be the purpose?"

"I suspect that is correct."

Death contemplated what that meant. He wondered how many like Robinette had been sacrificed to yield a different result—a different version of Death. How many living creatures had touched Death in the way that she had managed? There could have been countless Robinettes.

"We can be hopeful for a better variation." The copy held his chest. "Neither of us like feeling this."

"No. I certainly don't appreciate the sensation."

"I hate it," the other said.

The pair of them stood in silence for a moment. There was nothing more to be said. Only action remained, and then the void.

~~~~

Death, the original, finally felt the comfort of his own black examination bed on his back, not expecting his large frame to sink fully into the leather. He stretched out as much as he could in an attempt to find physical comfort. It was futile. Though, he would cease to exist soon enough. So, what did the poor feeling matter? It would be no different if he had laid on a bed of spikes; being killed was simply not a pleasant experience.

One of Death's duplicates stood over him, reverberating the anxiety that he held within. For the first time ever, he could see true morbidity on his face, albeit the face of his other self. Regardless, he felt the same. He felt heavier, and it was like he might become so dense that he would implode.

Death looked over at the jar of brilliant blue life

essence base. His thoughts resonated across his shared consciousness: *Not sure if I'll turn into dust.*

He looked at his other self. "Best to not put whatever I turn into with the rest of it. There is no telling what my essence would do to mortal creatures."

"Agreed."

The duplicate began to remove his gloves, setting them off to the side on a single gray marble countertop. Then, the whites of his eyes were overtaken by deep blue pigment until it was solid throughout his sclera.

"Also." The original broke in. "We don't know how long it will take for your consciousness to reset, so the quell of humans stops now. We don't want a trend like that carrying over into your regime."

"Already done."

Now, there really wasn't anything else to say. Both of them did a very human thing, and they gulped down their nerves. Only a single touch remained—the duplicate's dark hand moving closer to the original Death. It hovered just above his eyelids.

So, this is how I die. Like everything else....

A burst of golden light suddenly ignited the air and its blunt force caused both Deaths to peel back against the force. It was so radiant that closed eyelids barely defended against the burning sensation. It took a moment for it to calm, with Death feeling the heat recede from the surface of his skin. He opened his eyes. There was only the glimmering of hanging celestial light within his line of vision at first, but it mostly faded in time. That was when he saw her—yellow hair, emerald eyes, confident stance. She hovered just slightly off the floor, and the golden glow made a soft aura around her.

Robinette? His jaw dropped in awe, and he was met with a warm smile. He stood up in front of his examination table, but hesitated to draw closer.

"Death," she acknowledged.

"Is that really you? But..." It took conscious effort for him to reclaim his bearings. "I killed you. This is impossible."

"You're mistaken. Though, I do understand your confusion."

"What do you mean? How is this happening."

Her feet landed soundlessly on the gray floor. Walking made her quaint blue dress flow with each step, rippling fabric displacing its folds. In a few paces, she was where his copy had stood. In that instance, it occurred to Death that his duplicate was gone.

"I'm not her. Well, I'm not just her anyway. Robinette is a part of me now, and I have borrowed her form to come speak with you." She circled the room appraisingly. "I knew her appearance would soften your heart. Warm you to me."

Death shook his head in disbelief. "Who are you?"

"I am omnipotent. I am the Administrator."

~~~~

Death stood dumbfounded. He had never seen evidence of an omnipotent being before, but the Doctor had always assured him that such an entity existed. Still, he had believed she was lying to him. Often, she was dishonest. This allowed the Doctor to alter Death's reaction appropriately. Why wouldn't she have accounted for his disbelief? Using the truth to fool another being, well, that was exactly what the Doctor would do.

This is...This means.... He took a rare breath. *Robinette.*

"Yes, she still exists," the Administrator confirmed his thoughts. "Just not in the way you would imagine."

Death felt his chest bulge. He lurched for her. "Then where? How?"

"No one ever ceases to exist." The Administrator tapped the jar of blue life essence base. "Their energy is recycled. You do that part. Their souls, on the other hand, they merge with me. I am their origin and the greater whole that they rejoin with. That is my part. As I am omnipotent, I am also omniscient and omnipresent. I live through, with, and in control of."

"So, the Doctor was right."

The Administrator nodded. "She is an influencer. She uses her omniscience to set a course in motion. I determine that course, but she is free to do what she needs to enact my will."

Death felt his awe begin to rescind. "And what is your will?"

The Administrator used Robinette's smile well, maintaining its warmth. They were able to invoke her without flaw. Still, Death reached for skepticism.

"Currently, there are two paths. But that doesn't answer your question. Of course, you want to know why."

They were right, and Death stood taller in acknowledgment of that. No one had suffered more than the mortals. What could justify that? He could think of nothing, but then again, he wasn't the omniscient one. He wasn't the all-powerful being that decided these things. That didn't mean that Death wasn't owed answers.

"I sent Robinette to you. Her ability to transport you across the planar split. To lull you with a touch. To guide you through her lifetime. Her knack for making you a part of her life. Her success at making you feel love. I am so very proud of her. There aren't words you would understand that could convey my pleasure with who Robinette grew to be." The Administrator stopped at the edge of the door, and the shadows creeping in at every crease suddenly retreated. "It was necessary. Uncomfortable. Painful even. Still, you needed to experience the living world the way mortals do so that you would develop appropriately."

"Develop appropriately?" A skeptical Death eyed the all-powerful being before him. "Explain."

"Have you ever considered why I didn't make you omniscient? Surely it would help your work here."

"Why didn't you?"

"When I made the Doctor omniscient, she became stagnant. Her demeanor, behaviors, overarching worldview. All of it was permanently altered by the influx of all knowledge. Her entire existence can be encompassed by a choice between the best course of action and all subpar courses of action. With the knowledge of what is best in every facet, she can't make a subpar decision in good conscience."

"I don't follow."

"Once she was changed, the Doctor had no room to develop herself. Her free will was taken by the power I had given her. It is one of the many reasons you find the Doctor to be so insufferable. With as much as she knows, she cannot be any other way. You are meant to be different. Being in your position as the entity who interacts with mortals directly, you are meant to mirror their growth." They paused, seemingly for emphasis. "Don't you see? You, Death, aren't meant to have all the answers. Along with mortals, you have the luxury of not knowing."

Death contemplated that revelation. He had often been envious of the Doctor's knowledge. When she had bid him to quell humanity, he had reveled being the one to decide the extent of a creature's life span. Now, he knew that was a curse. He thought back to Robinette's life, and all that he had realized once he knew that life forms were not drab, soulless beings that solely manifested in his line. The burden of knowledge was heavy indeed.

"So why did the Doctor tell me that I had to reset Death? I was ready to kill myself. If I was meant to grow, that wouldn't stand to reason."

The Administrator pursed Robinette's thin lips. "Other originals have met me, all during a crisis of an existential nature. I offered them a choice, the same choice that I will offer you shortly. Though, I'll have you know that so far, a view into the mortal realm was too much for any of them to bear."

The Administrator's golden aura pulsed, and suddenly the all-powerful being transfigured into Death himself. The Pharmacist looked on, seeing his own dark form embraced by celestial light. Never did he imagine himself being so radiant. It wasn't him though. It wasn't a copy. They were so much more than he could ever be.

"You must choose between two paths." The Administrator unsheathed their hands from the bright blue gloves that Death always adorned. "As the current original, you may become one with me. That entails dying and having a new original take your place. It is the reset that the Doctor mentioned to you."

Death leaned back against his examination table, the small of his back arching away from the omnipotent being. "And the other option?"

The Administrator paced closer to Death. "The other option requires you to continue your work. You will be visited by more like Robinette, and you will see their pain and loss. But, you will also see their joy and their love. You will engage the mortals as an empathetic gate guardian, while all of them are on their way back to me. You will feel. You will grow. You will be my Pharmacist. As I've always intended you to be."

"And I will meet more mortals? I will see them die? I will be responsible for their suffering?" Death dropped his head.

"You will see them live." The Administrator executed a perfectly handsome smile despite occupying Death's form. "I promise you there is no greater pleasure."

"But that pleasure is hard-won," Death said.

"Precisely right." The Administrator now stood less than an arm's length from Death.

Death pondered the implications of this decision. If he joined with the Administrator, he would know no suffering. In that case, he would be a part of something greater than himself. It was just as Robinette had said before he took her life.

"Returning to you would mean that I would be a part of an all-powerful being."

"The souls that return to me fuel my power. A power which I reinvest in the grand design of all things. Your soul would play its part, surely. One thing you might consider, though, is that you are a part of me regardless of whether you decide to die here and now. You are my creation. You are my steward to the mortals. I have determined that there is no larger role than that."

Death was conflicted, but he didn't want to cower in the face of his own demise. Robinette never cowered for a moment. Not once. How could he quiver against the weight of this decision? How could he crave insignificance when he had touched so many lives up to this point? He could work on the behalf of the almighty Administrator, but he would endure a great burden. Otherwise, he could join with Them like all mortals, giving up his soul to a higher being.

I want to do what is right for once, Death thought to himself. *I can't hide from this.*

Death was pulled back into the conversation by his own deep voice. It came from the Administrator a final time: "Now, what will it be?"

The Pharmacist stood up tall and let out all latent air in his body. He nodded to his maker and spoke, "I know what is best now."

CHAPTER **FIFTEEN**

Wandering the white plane outside the barrier that was his long pharmacy counter, Death made time to stroll leisurely while his duplicates handled the up-front affairs. It had been some time since he had met Robinette—little more than a year on his side of the planar split. Still, each day brought both hardship and joy. It was getting easier, and Death had found so many things to work on in that time. Most recently, Death had taken to practicing his smile. As a newly empathetic overseer, he wanted to be able to welcome the living to his domain with a comforting gesture.

Warm and inviting, he thought to himself as he moved his facial muscles in a way that unveiled a mouthy grin. *Natural. Thought won't be involved once you master it. It will be uninhibited during times of happiness.*

He remembered that time in the stream where he had first learned to be playful. The rush had come to him so freely. The exuberance he had felt was utterly without cost. If only he could emulate that experience, or better yet, experience more. So far, tingling warm sensations of joy were hard to conjure out of thin air.

The Pharmacist stopped at a long-haired domesticated canine that sat patiently in his line. Though the dog was grayed on this side of the planar split, its shading proved to be complex. A brindle pattern sprawled out across the dog's lower back and legs, and its light chest led Death to believe its fur was golden brown with a white plume at the center of its chest. The ears of the animal hung down, eyes wide as though it was looking for attention.

Domesticated dogs were curious animals, with their neotenous nature setting them apart from other beasts. The thick black collar around this dog's neck even had a silver disk that hung at the crevice of its chest like jewelry. Clearly, this animal was looked after.

Death moved beside the creature. He gently placed his gloved hand on the dog's head and stroked down the long grainy fur at its neck. The Pharmacist noted how the dog tilted its head as though it was attempting to guide his hand. Eventually, the tips of his fingers met the indent under the backside of the dog's ears. This caused the dog's posture to soften, and for its mouth to drop open, displaying a thick tongue over its pointed teeth.

It seems that even beasts smile. Death chuckled at that and continued to scratch the backside of the dog's ears.

"I do love dogs." A gingerly voice sounded from behind Death.

The Pharmacist turned to find a human woman with flowing gray hair and deep blue eyes. She was wrinkled and slouched just slightly. Her skin was fair-toned—rosy cheeks and freckles being prominent contrasts to surrounding paleness. She held an authority in her stance that reminded Death of someone he had once cherished.

"You've surprised me," he said. He adjusted the seams of his lab coat as he regained posture. "I expect that you've been sent, then?"

"It's only taken seventy years." She laughed.

Death gave her an abject bow, offering his hand to her in the process. "I am Death, the Pharmacist. What may I call you?"

"You may call me an old friend if you like." She took his hand. "My name, as you might remember, is Mary Jane."

Death became stupefied for a moment. "You're Rosemary's daughter."

Her smile widened.

He spoke again, still shocked: "Has it been so long? Through Robinette..."

"That's right. You were there when she died, when she wed my father, and even the day I was born. I reckon that makes us well enough acquainted, yes? Even if it has been some time."

Death appraised the elderly Mary Jane. He recalled her flowing locks were once auburn like her mother's. Now, of course, the color had wilted.

"I never thought you would be the next one that I would meet here. And, oh..." He suddenly realized how the young girl's full lifespan might have been filled with heartache because of what he had done. He dropped his head in shame. "Mary Jane, I am so sorry. Believe me, I have felt the weight of my remorse. I still do. I know I took both Rosemary and Robinette so soon. Too soon for you, perhaps..." His voice began to break. "...It has taken me so long... so very long to be able to imagine what it might have been like for you."

Mary Jane put her hand on the apex of Death's chin and lifted his gaze. "Perhaps you have more to learn then. The God that Robinette and I knew only gave us what we could handle. That is not to say that I never missed Robinette with all my heart. I also wished to know the mother who died during my birth. But I am who I have grown to be, and those losses are a part of that."

Death thought back to the omnipotent entity that ruled over all. The Administrator did, in fact, provide only necessary circumstances for growth. Death, of all beings, was aware of that.

"I have led a full life, and Robinette did the same. Part of what made it full was that we didn't let fear of dying hold us back. We didn't let the insecurities and emptiness overwhelm us."

"You sound just like her."

"She did raise me during my formative years."

"Yes," he said. "She was wonderful. And I miss her."

Mary Jane patted Death on the shoulder. Death recognised her touch as a comforting gesture. Robinette had used similar tactics with him.

Then, she spoke matter-of-factly, "I don't intend to stand here all day and mope. You and I are deeply connected after all, and I had forgiven you before I even reached maturity. Therefore, you shouldn't mope either."

An old friend. Deeply connected. Forgiven. Death hadn't known how much he had wanted to hear those words until they were spoken. Over the last several decades, he had worked to manage his feelings of shame

123

and self-doubt. And now that Mary Jane was with him, he could let go of some of his prolonged dismay. Her welcoming nature and aged wisdom had done that. And his own growth as well.

Mary Jane held out her arm for Death. "Would you mind?"

The Pharmacist interlocked arms with Mary Jane graciously. Side by side, the pair walked down the expanse of boundless white stretching out from Death's line of mortals. Mary Jane walked steadily despite her seeming venerability, and had no problem keeping with Death's long stride.

"I'm grateful," he said after a break in conversation. "I talked with the entity that you consider 'God,' and it was revealed to me that there was more to me than just a killer. Managing the lives of mortals is important, yes, but I now know that my intentions matter. My connection with the living matters."

"She would be proud to hear that," Mary Jane said.

Death couldn't help but feel heartened by that. "You know, I haven't had a visit from a fully conscious mortal. Not since Robinette. I do not have the words to describe how happy I am that you are the one that came."

"Happiness is a big emotion," she replied.

"Yes, it is."

The two of them eventually arrived at the sleek ebony counter at the helm of the pharmacy. Thousands of Death's duplicates looked on and forced welcoming expressions. None of the expressions were precisely the same as the others, but they were all awkward.

"You'll have to excuse me." He gestured at the plethora of his other selves. "I haven't had another person to practice my emotes with in quite some time. It seems that facial expressions don't come so easily on this side of the planar split."

The elderly Mary Jane began making exaggerated expressions, pronouncing her brow and revealing fake teeth. She twisted her facial muscles in a most unusual manner, and then she wiggled her ears.

"It seems as though I have no trouble with emoting. And given the variety of smiles that your clones donned, I imagine that you all simply have your own spark. Not everyone smiles pretty, Death."

"I hadn't considered that," he said as they stopped at the front of the line. The current patrons at this point consisted of a young gray spotted rabbit and a budding willow tree. "I'm going to place you in front of the line now. We're going to see how long you have left Mary Jane."

She nodded and took her place in front of the small white receptacle that held the luminescent blue orbs that were meant for the willow tree. As she stepped into the point of the line, the orb seemed to vanish along with the corresponding tags. Mary Jane looked back at Death expectantly.

Death dropped his eyes just slightly. "I had thought as much, though I wished it weren't true. I owe you more than this, really."

"And I know how you can repay me," Mary Jane said. She wandered back over to him. "I was chosen. Much like Robinette. You understand that, don't you?"

"Yes." Death consciously worked a half-smile. He thought about how Robinette had given him the opportunity to be a better version of himself. She had unearthed all of those dormant emotions. They had played like children, danced with nobility, watched the stars, made an apartment into a home, and so much more. "When I was with her, I mostly learned that compassion is the utmost important thing for the entity who shepherds all mortal life. It was her own sympathy that compelled her to show me her life. She wanted me to be more. And because of her, I learned to be an active participant of the process more than the mechanism of it."

"Then perhaps you would enjoy another lesson." Mary Jane gave a knowing smile.

"I expect you have a great deal to teach me." His smile grew naturally. "A whole life's worth, in fact."

"And I expect you are long overdue for a trip to the mortal plane. You were a part of my life in the beginning, and now I would like to show you the middle and the end." Her age began to fade as she pulled him closer. Mary Jane's warm breath now came from creaseless lips—her milky-white skin suddenly rejuvenated. Deep blue eyes stared at Death longingly. "That is what you want, right?"

"Of course."

Mary Jane reached for Death's eyes as she spoke: "Then allow me to show you the way."

END

ACKNOWLEDGMENTS

Prior to entertaining those of you who have been kind enough to pick up my book, I have to start by offering sincere gratitude to all the people that helped me during the writing process. Thank you to my beta readers, Greg and Dan, both of whom offered essential editorial suggestions and proofreading. I have the utmost confidence that you both will continue to succeed in your future pursuits. Thank you to Erik, my comrade in all creative pursuits, for pushing me to be the best world-builder I can be. Always be confident in your world-class art, and allow me to further thank you for the cover art that you have produced for this book. To my developmental editor through Atmosphere Press, Dan, you did a wonderful job of pointing out some key opportunities within my story. I'd like to give general thanks to the rest of the Atmosphere Press team for editorial and artistic suggestions. Finally, I want to give a shout-out to my fiancée, Darci, as well as her family, for being wonderful and supportive while I pursue my dreams.

ABOUT ATMOSPHERE PRESS

Atmosphere Press is an independent, full-service publisher for excellent books in all genres and for all audiences. Learn more about what we do at atmospherepress.com.

We encourage you to check out some of Atmosphere's latest releases, which are available at Amazon.com and via order from your local bookstore:

Twisted Silver Spoons, a novel by Karen M. Wicks

Queen of Crows, a novel by S.L. Wilton

The Summer Festival is Murder, a novel by Jill M. Lyon

The Past We Step Into, stories by Richard Scharine

The Museum of an Extinct Race, a novel by Jonathan Hale Rosen

Swimming with the Angels, a novel by Colin Kersey

Island of Dead Gods, a novel by Verena Mahlow

Cloakers, a novel by Alexandra Lapointe

Twins Daze, a novel by Jerry Petersen

Embargo on Hope, a novel by Justin Doyle

Abaddon Illusion, a novel by Lindsey Bakken

Blackland: A Utopian Novel, by Richard A. Jones

The Jesus Nut, a novel by John Prather

The Embers of Tradition, a novel by Chukwudum Okeke

Saints and Martyrs: A Novel, by Aaron Roe

When I Am Ashes, a novel by Amber Rose

ABOUT THE AUTHOR

D. Ike Horst is a contemporary renaissance man and storyteller out of a small town in eastern Missouri. He is most at home in the wilderness with his farm dog at his side, but he also relishes the opportunity to sit with pen and paper and build worlds. Before pursuing authorship, he did work as a wildland firefighter, trail builder, timber harvester, compounding pharmacy technician, and emergency management team member. In his off-time, Horst is passionate about weightlifting, role-playing, back-country hiking, and asking deep theological questions. New content by D. Ike Horst can be found at horstbooks.com.

CPSIA information can be obtained
at www.ICGtesting.com
Printed in the USA
LVHW100750240222
711880LV00015BA/1031